A Guitar Case

A Guitar Case

The Adventures of Ben, Angie & Red Brown

By Carl M. Grefenstette

Howard —
Whenever I think
of you I remember
that fabulous SG Special!

Carl

Library of Congress Cataloging-in-Publication Data is available upon request.
Grefenstette, Carl M.
A Guitar Case: The Adventures of Ben, Angie and Red Brown

ISBN-13: 9781099754791

Cover Design: Carl Grefenstette and Group 2
Cover Photo: Abalone Vintage

To Ben and Angie, Wherever they are.
And to Karen
Where she is.

Chapter One

Ben didn't know what to expect. The last time he had spoken to Aunt Maggie was over thirty years ago.

At a family reunion in South Park.

Aunts, uncles and cousins were all posing for a picture, mimicking a photo they took at the exact same spot ten years earlier. Once again he was sitting next to his dad's sister, Aunt Maggie. He didn't have much to say. She was more than twenty years older than he was. And when you're only 18 someone over 40 is pretty ancient.

But when she mentioned music, Ben told her about his band. "*The Static* – Available for Parties, Weddings & All Around Good Times." He was surprised when she asked what kind of guitar he played. "A Gibson Melody Maker," he said, "And a Harmony Sovereign H1260. The same model used by John Sebastian at Woodstock!" He often mentioned the Woodstock connection back then, when people still cared about the event. It wasn't until the 1990s that he learned that Jimmy Page also used an H1260 with Led Zeppelin. That would have made a much hipper story, but by the 90s Ben had long stopped playing.

A few minutes later the photo was taken, and Ben and Aunt Maggie moved on to mingle with their respective family age groups. After the reunion Maggie returned to her home in Florida, and Ben had so many other local aunts and uncles that she rarely crossed his mind.

In fact, he almost had to be reminded who she was when he learned that she had passed away peacefully a month ago. And before long she again faded in his memory.

So the phone call from a lawyer in Florida came as quite a surprise.

"Mr. Benjamin Cooper? This is Marcus Turner of Turner & Associates in Miami."

Ben wasn't quite sure what this had to do with him, but he listened.

"My firm is handling your aunt's estate."

Estate?

"As you are aware, your aunt was quite a musician in her early days…"

No, he wasn't aware.

"… and she left specific instructions that you were to get her favorite guitar. We'd like to ship it to you today."

"OK, thanks." The best reply he could think of.

Ben was a bit taken aback. And intrigued. He had no idea Aunt Maggie played guitar. And he was shocked that she apparently remembered their conversation all those decades ago.

And another feeling was stirring inside him.

It had been years since he even strummed a guitar. *The Static* fizzled out in the early 1980s, as band members got married and needed "real" jobs to raise their families. He jammed with a few other folks, but merely playing in the basement grew frustrating. His youthful enthusiasm and the dream of making it big began to wane. When he married Jane in 1983 and landed a job with Bismark Insurance, he put the guitars away.

The marriage lasted for ten years, some good, some bad. Climbing the corporate ladder seemed to take forever. And very little of that was good. Now, in his late-50s, Ben was exhausted. And there was no music in his life. He wasn't even sure where his guitars were. The Harmony was probably in a closet in the basement. The Melody Maker might be at his parents' house.

When he thought of the mystery guitar on its way from Florida, he noticed his blood racing a little faster. Suddenly life became more interesting. He flashed back to the day his mom bought him the Melody Maker. Ben had been taking lessons at Victor J. Lawrence Music Studios in the South Hills, and Victor let his students use the Melody Maker for their lessons. One day Victor offered the guitar for sale. The price was high, $175, and to this day Ben isn't sure how his mother could afford it. But she bought the guitar, and it was the happiest day of his life.

Ben had heard of the Gibson brand name, but he knew little of its history. The only reason he knew the model name of his new guitar was because the words "Melody Maker" were stamped in white letters on the pickguard between the neck pickup and the end of the fingerboard.

When he asked about other Gibson models, Victor gave him a beautiful color Gibson catalog, full of stunning guitars. Oddly, the guitar listed as a Melody Maker didn't match Ben's at all. Then, a month later, a kid down the street bought a used Melody Maker from another store. That one looked more like Ben's than the one pictured in the catalog, but it was still a bit off. He was intrigued by these inconsistencies. Three guitars, all labeled "Melody Maker," but all different. One thing was sure, though. The guitar played like a dream.

Now, years later, he didn't even know where it was.

Deep inside, though, the fascination was still there. He had no idea what kind of guitar Aunt Maggie was sending him. But his mind was flooding with memories of the guitars he played when he was young. The different shapes and colors. The different models and different sounds. Ben was very successful in the business world. But he couldn't remember the last time he felt something mysterious and magical; the way he felt when he held that Melody Maker. The pending delivery was not only bringing a guitar, it was renewing age-old feelings and interests.

He could hardly wait.

Chapter Two

Ben was surprised when he saw the box.

When he heard that Aunt Maggie left him a guitar in her will, he presumed it would be an acoustic. No particular reason. He just pictured an aging old lady sitting on her couch, strumming folk songs.

But this box was clearly too thin.

It was leaning against a bookshelf on the other side of his office at Bismark Insurance. FedEx regularly delivered to Bismark, but this package was certainly larger than the usual overnight paperwork.

Ben lived in a quiet suburban neighborhood, but given the randomness of Pittsburgh weather he thought it was wise to have the guitar delivered to his office. Now it was a constant distraction as he glanced up from his paperwork every few minutes to stare at the mystery box.

***

A few hours later he was home, still staring at the box, which was now leaning against the couch in his living room.

When he opened it, the first thing visible was the frayed brown leather end-piece of a hardshell case. As he eased the rectangular case from the tight fitting box, he could see that it was a dark orange tweed.

Although it had been years since Ben had picked up a guitar, he had seen tweed cases before. Maybe on TV, or perhaps being carried by musicians around town. But this one was different. It was shiny, as if it had a clear coat of finish on it, and it was much, much darker than the yellow tweed he had seen before. "I'm no expert," he lightheartedly said to himself, "but this is old!"

He gently set the case on his dining room table, and opened it. It was a Stratocaster. He was familiar with the model. But just like the case, it had a different look to it. The colors were very faded, from dark brown on the edges to a pale yellow, almost natural wood color in the center. "'Starburst'," he thought; and then he immediately corrected himself, "no, it's called 'sunburst'." The pickguard looked like a thin piece of white plastic. And one of the pickups seemed to have a black spot on the bottom edge. When he looked closer, the white plastic covering the pickup was actually broken.

He went right to his computer.

Googling "Fender Stratocaster" turned up almost three million links. The first one was the Fender company website, so he searched there. He was surprised to see that Fender had over 100 different types of new Stratocasters on their site. That didn't help. He tried Wikipedia, which explained that the earliest Stratocasters had "two-tone sunburst" finishes. That was good. Unfortunately, the info then jumped through the years pretty rapidly. Finally he found a web site that listed serial numbers. His was 13350, which seemed to indicate it was made in 1956. But he knew he was in over his head.

From Ben's years in corporate America (and from watching the TV show *Pawn Stars*) he decided that he should call in an expert. He remembered a store he had visited in the early 1980s, right before his band broke up. The name was easy enough to remember, Pittsburgh Guitars. He Googled them. He was impressed. They were still in business. Anyone who has been around *that* long must know what they're talking about. He decided to head there first thing in the morning.

***

Later that evening, as he thought about the guitar over his usual glass of wine, different topics ran through his head. Is it really as old as he suspects? And if so, is it valuable? And if it's valuable, should he sell it?

He remembered that last year, while going through the pockets of a very old jacket he was donating to Goodwill, he had found a guitar pick. Now he rummaged through his kitchen junk drawer and found the pick. White with a faded 'M' for Medium imprinted on it. Back in his band days he had always favored medium gauge picks. And although they came in a variety of colors, he liked that the white ones were easier to find if you dropped them on a darkened stage.

He picked up the guitar and strummed a few chords. It felt really good. He played a couple of songs he remembered from the old days, and even without being plugged into an amp, the guitar rang out. He liked that.

Ben didn't know if the guitar actually worked, and had no way to try it, since he had sold his amp decades ago. The Fender Twin Reverb seemed to get heavier every year, although, of course, that was just him aging. He got rid of it because seeing the amp sitting there idle was just as depressing as trying to lift it.

But working or not, he was impressed with the Stratocaster. And it was a gift from a late aunt. Admittedly an aunt he hadn't spoken to in years, which made it a bit mysterious. But still, it *was* a gift. Ben decided to keep it.

***

The next morning he called his office and took a vacation day. The excitement of having a guitar back in his life merited it. A little after 10 am he headed to Pittsburgh Guitars. When he arrived, tweed case in hand, he was surprised to see that they weren't open yet. The old 19th century building had a recessed entranceway, so he was protected from the winter weather. He decided to wait.

As he watched the variety of folks passing by in either direction on the sidewalk, he felt a bit odd to be out of the office during business hours. As if he were playing hooky from school.

Ten minutes later a woman came running through the busy traffic in front of the store, with a Starbucks cup in her hand. She was dressed for the weather with black gloves and a beige jacket and her hair was pulled up under a wool cap. As she joined him in the store entranceway she nodded slightly as a casual way to say hello. He was struck by her light blue eyes. They had a certain confidence to them. The kind of confidence that would start a conversation with a complete stranger.

"The line was shorter than I expected," she said holding up the cup, "so I'm a little early, too."

Looking at the case, she added, "An old Strat, I presume."

Ben was surprised, both at her friendliness and apparent accuracy.

"Yes." He replied. "At least I *think* it's old…"

"Well, the case is right," she quickly offered. Pointing at the still locked door, she said, "These guys will set you straight. They know a lot more than both of us put together."

She continued, "I'm Angie, by the way."

"Hi, I'm Ben. Are you a musician?"

"Not much of one," she replied, sipping her coffee. "I'm just here to pick up a repair. Do you have a lot of guitars?"

"I have an old Melody Maker, but I don't know when that was made either."

"Well, it's simple enough to narrow it down. What color is it?"

"Red," said Ben, intrigued that she could guess the age of a guitar even he hadn't seen in years.

"Is it see-through red, or solid red?" she asked.

8

When she saw the confused look on his face, she added, "Can you see the grain through the finish?"

"I think so…" he said, still unsure.

"Okay, if you're not sure, let's approach it a different way," she said. "What color is the pickguard?"

That one he knew. "Black!"

"Then it was made between 1963 and 1965," she said matter-of-factly.

Ben was stunned.

"Really? How do you know?"

"It's a pretty easy one," Angie explained. "They made four versions of the Melody Maker back in the 60s and they all had different features. I presume it's from the 60s, since you said *old*."

He nodded. "Yeah, I got it in 1973, but it was used by a guitar teacher for years. I know it's older."

She continued, "The first Melody Makers in 1959 were single cutaway, like a super skinny Les Paul Junior. They probably used the same template and just cut a thinner piece of mahogany. In '61, they changed it to a double cutaway. Everybody was going double-cutaway around '60, '61."

She was almost going too fast. But he followed along, fascinated.

"In 1963, for some reason they modified the body shape. It was still a double-cutaway, but the horns got bigger and the back-end of the body got thinner."

Angie held up her hands, one of them still holding the coffee cup, and outlined the two body shapes in the air.

"So, those are the first three," she said, counting them out with her gloved fingers as she spoke, "Les Paul-ish single cut, same shape double-cut, and then kind of a squashed back-end version."

"And the fourth?" asked Ben.

9

"In 1965, they changed it to mimic an SG body, with contoured edges and pointier points."

He laughed at "pointier points."

"The colors help date yours," she continued.

He was getting a miniature guitar history lecture right here on the sidewalk. Except Ben was enjoying this far more than any lecture he had ever attended. Both in topic, and lecturer.

"Melody Maker versions one and two had sunburst finishes, just like the Les Paul Juniors they were modeled after. If yours is red then you don't have one of those."

"Okay, not one or two," he said.

"Right," she said. "Then, with version three they changed to see-through red, kinda like an SG of the era, only not as dark. And version four, the ones that were shaped just like SGs, were solid colors, either red or blue. When you weren't sure about the type of red, I asked about the pickguard, because version three had a black pickguard, just like all of the Melody Makers before it, and version four switched to a white pickguard."

She hesitated for a second, and then, as if to complete the description, she added, "...and white pickup covers."

Ben smiled, not knowing how to respond. Then he remembered the catalog Victor Lawrence gave him forty-five years ago.

"So that's why my guitar didn't match the Melody Maker in the catalog..." he said, almost to himself.

"Was it a really nice color Gibson catalog?" Angie asked.

"Yes," he said, amazed. "How did you know?"

She smiled. "You're talking about Gibson's 1966 catalog. The one with the green trees on the cover, right? They made so much money during the `64-`65 guitar boom that in `66 they came out with their finest

10

catalog ever. And they made a ton of them. It's really one of the nicest catalogs I've ever seen."

His mind was spinning. She continued, "That catalog has version four Melody Makers, the ones with the SG body, the solid-colors, and the white pickguard."

"Right!" he exclaimed. "I remember the pickguard in the catalog was white!"

Simultaneously, he flashed back to the Melody Maker that the kid down the street had. Ben had always wondered why it didn't quite match his. The one down the street was sunburst! And the points were just slightly smaller, and the back slightly wider. That kid had the second version. Ben's was the third!

He was about to thank Angie for solving years of childhood confusion, when the door opened and Sam from Pittsburgh Guitars said, "Come on in outta the cold!"

Angie walked into the store, searching her pocket for her repair claim check, while waving back at Ben, "Nice chatting with ya, Ben."

"Yeah," he said hesitantly, as she turned away from him.

He was still standing at the doorway, stunned by the conversation, when Sam's voice brought him back to reality, "What can we do for you? Did you come to sell us your Strat?"

"Oh, no," Ben said. "It's a family heirloom. I just want it checked out."

"No problem," said Sam. "Let's take a look."

Pittsburgh Guitars was in a ten-block neighborhood of three and four story buildings from the late 1800s, with retail shops on the first floor and apartments above. The walls of the guitar store were lined with several hundred electric and acoustic guitars, basses and even ukuleles. In front of the guitars, for the first third of the store, were glass display cases full of pedals, microphones and other small items.

Sam pointed toward the first display case, its top covered with a felt pad. "Put it right up here on the counter."

Ben laid the case on the pad, undid the latches and opened it.

Looking down at the guitar Sam smiled and said, "Nice!" As he lifted it out of the case, he said, "What is it, a `56?" He quickly spun it around, looked at the serial number, and said, "Yep, `56."

Sam walked over to a row of amplifiers and plugged it in. The first chord he played sounded heavenly. Ben smiled. Sam moved the toggle switch from the back position to the front. Now it was more mellow and rich sounding. "It's a classic," said Sam as he played a few licks. When he moved the toggle to the middle position, though, the sound stopped. Sam jiggled the switch a bit, checking for a bad connection, but still no sound.

That's bad, Ben thought. But Sam's demeanor calmed him.

"No problem," he assured Ben. "I'm sure you want our repairman Scott to look under the pickguard anyway, to see if everything is original. It's possible that the pickup is bad. But if it is, we can have it re-wound. And it could be as simple as a loose solder connection."

As Sam was writing up the repair tag, Ben asked, "What do you think it's worth?"

"Well," said Sam, casually, "Let's start with *a lot*. But we should wait to see if it's all original. That heavily factors into the value."

As he was giving Sam his name and phone number, out of the corner of his eye Ben could see Angie at the cash register paying John, the store's owner, for the repair bill on her guitar. He turned toward her, just as she looked up. "Nice Strat," she said, "Sounds great." Turning toward the door, her guitar in hand, she added, "See ya around."

Sam handed Ben the claim check, and said, "I'll try to have Scott do this today. We'll call you tonight."

"Thanks," said Ben.

Then, acting as if it were an afterthought, he added, "Do you know that girl who just left?"

He couldn't decide whether to refer to her as a "girl" or "woman." He guessed she was twenty years younger than him, but that would still put her in her late-thirties. At Bismark Insurance, many of his co-workers were women. And in the business world, "woman" is the only acceptable term. But somehow, in this guitar store, the world seemed younger and more light-hearted. It seemed perfectly appropriate to refer to Angie as a "girl."

Glancing toward the door, Sam replied, "Oh, sure. That's Angie. She's a regular."

"She knows a lot about guitars," said Ben, glancing around at the hundreds of instruments hanging on the wall. "It's an interesting topic."

"Well, that's all we talk about around here," said Sam, as he turned to a newly arriving customer. "We'll call you later, Ben."

***

Ben drove home in silence. He'd usually listen to the radio or make phone calls. Today's events, though, shook him up. His regular work day was full of numbers and dates and facts and spreadsheets. He was used to dealing with a lot of data. But listening to Angie rattle off the dates and changes to the different Melody Maker guitars was quite enjoyable. And although he didn't know much about Gibson's other models, he did know that the Melody Maker was one of the cheapest guitars Gibson made. It couldn't have much significance in the history of vintage guitars. Imagine the *other* stories out there. There are thousands of guitar models. Do they all have detailed stories and histories? They must!

He decided to drive right to his parents' house, and look for his Melody Maker. He wanted to examine the color and shape. He wanted to remember everything Angie told him. He wanted to know all of those dates and versions of the Melody Makers. And he wanted to find that old Gibson catalog. And learn more guitar stories.

Before he got to his parents' house, though, his cell phone rang. It was Scott.

"Ben, I took your guitar apart to check the wiring. The middle pickup isn't bad, and the wiring wasn't loose. It was intentionally disconnected."

Ben wondered what that would mean...

Scott continued, "It's as if someone wanted you to go in there, to fix it. And here's the strange part..."

"What?" asked Ben.

"Under the toggle switch, right where the wires were disconnected, was a small, folded envelope. Addressed to you."

Chapter Three

Ben ran up the steps in front of his parents' house. Two at a time, the way he used to, forty years ago.

"Mom, do you know where my old red guitar is?"

"Nice to see you, too, Ben," his mother light-heartedly said from the living room couch.

"Sorry. Hi, mom. Hi, dad," he said.

His dad, sitting on the same couch, watching TV, looked up and waved. Ben continued, "And remember my box of music books? Have you seen that?"

"I think the box is in the attic," his mother replied, "And your guitar is under the bed in the guest room…"

Ben immediately turned toward his old bedroom, smiling to himself as he always did when they called it the "guest room."

Halfway down the hallway he raised his voice to ask yet another question to his parents back in the living room, "And did you know Aunt Maggie played guitar?"

Ben slid the guitar case from under the bed. When he saw the rectangular hard case he remembered the guitar's original one, made of black heavy-duty cardboard. The original case fell apart after being loaded into the van one too many times when his band was playing regularly. He tried to buy a Gibson Les Paul case, but the Melody Maker wouldn't fit, so he ended up with a rectangular Japanese-made case.

He wiped the dust from the top and opened the case. Sure enough, he could see the wood grain through the red finish. See-through red, just as Angie had predicted.

Ben lifted the guitar from the case and strummed an A chord, the first chord he had ever learned. He smiled. To his surprise the guitar was still mostly in tune.

He put the guitar back in the case, picked it up and walked back to the living room.

His dad turned from the TV and said, "Maggie was always away singing with her band. I think I have their picture around here somewhere."

His mother also turned and said, "Can we get that picture for you later, honey? We'll get the box, too." Turning back to the TV, she added, "Come back for dinner. Our show is coming on now."

Ben understood. She had been watching the *The Young And The Restless* for as long as he could remember, and when his dad retired he got hooked on it too. This was not the right time of day to be asking questions.

He smiled again, though, when "Victor" appeared on the screen. He remembered seeing that same actor as a World War II German soldier on *Rat Patrol,* a TV show Ben used to watch when he was nine years old. "Man, that guy's had a long career!" he said to himself.

On the way out the door he said, "I'll see you at dinner!"

***

Ben hadn't planned on driving back and forth across town on his day off, but he decided to head straight back to Pittsburgh Guitars. The Stratocaster from Aunt Maggie became even more interesting when Scott found a note inside the guitar. Especially since the note was addressed to Ben.

***

Now familiar with Pittsburgh Guitars, Ben walked right in and put his Melody Maker case on the counter.

"Welcome back!" said Sam. "What did you bring us now?"

"My Melody Maker," said Ben. "Not for sale."

"What year?" Sam asked, as he opened the case. Then, without waiting for Ben to answer, Sam continued, "Cool! A `64."

Just as he had been earlier, during his conversation with Angie, Ben was amazed. These guitar people were really passionate about their field.

Sam played a chord and then reached up to the headstock to tune the D-string. He looked back at Ben. "It could be a late `63, or early `65. It's really hard to tell with the serial numbers from that era. But it's definitely a circa-`64 guitar. Would you like to have Scott set this one up, too?"

"Yeah," said Ben. "And he called to say the Stratocaster is ready."

Just then Scott rounded the corner from the repair shop carrying the orange-ish tweed case.

"Oh, hi, Ben. The Strat looks great!" said Scott. "It was made on March 6, 1956 and it's 100% original."

"That'll be $45 plus tax for the set-up," Scott continued. "And no charge for the letter delivery," he said, as he handed Ben a small, folded envelope.

Ben was temporarily speechless. He had too many questions rattling through his head to even get one out.

"100% original is good, right?" Ben asked, even though he knew it was a foolish question.

"Oh yeah," said Scott.

"Any idea what it's worth?" Ben asked quietly.

Scott said, "Well, it's got a lotta wear, but it's legitimate play-wear…no refinishing or anything. And it has a great vibe. I'd say it would at least be in the $20- or $22,000 range. Maybe a little more."

The figure shocked Ben even more than the mystery note that was hidden inside. Twenty thousand dollars. That's a long way from the $175 his mother paid for the Melody Maker.

"Thanks...thanks," Ben said nervously as he shook Scott's hand.

"Don't forget," Scott added, "If you ever want to sell it..."

"I know, I know. I'll bring it here," said Ben, "But I won't. Sell it, that is."

In a bit of a daze he handed Sam his credit card. He barely paid attention as Sam handed him the receipt. He couldn't get over Aunt Maggie's generosity. And the value of the guitar! As he regained his composure, he saw that Scott had picked up the Melody Maker and was looking it over.

"What about that one?" he asked.

While nonchalantly playing the intro to "Something" by The Beatles on the red guitar, Scott replied, "Well, we should look inside, but at first glance it looks all-original, too. I've seen people asking as much as $2,000 for these, but $1,500 is a more realistic price."

Not as valuable as the Strat, but still impressive. Ben wondered if he should have been buying guitars for the last twenty years, instead of putting his money into the stock market.

As Sam wrote up a repair tag for the Melody Maker, Ben asked, "Do you mind if I hang out for a bit?"

"Not a problem!" said Sam, safely stashing both guitars behind the counter.

Ben went to the back of the room, sat down, and tried to make sense of his day so far. Then he remembered the note in his pocket.

As Sam directed his attention to other customers, Ben slowly unfolded the envelope and opened it. Inside was a small piece of stationary. Written in the beautiful, flowing handwriting of someone who learned to write in cursive in the 1940s, was a message from Aunt Maggie. It read:

> *Dear Benjamin,*
>
> *Please help Red with his guitar. It might be valuable.*
>
> *Mr. Bassman will know where he is.*
>
> *Love, Maggie*
>
> *PS: I hope you like the Strat*

Ben stared at the letter. He had never heard of "Red," and he had no idea who "Mr. Bassman" was. Heck, he didn't even know Aunt Maggie played guitar until last week. Who were these people? Why was the letter so vague? And why was it hidden in a guitar?

A rickety van pulled up out front and a traveling band came in to buy extra strings and cables. A couple of college students bought ukuleles. Two guitar students, a kid around twelve and a middle-aged woman, entered the store and then headed to different lesson rooms with their respective guitar teachers. All while Ben sat there, thinking about the letter.

He hardly considered himself a detective, but he tried to analyze what little info he had. First of all, the letter was vague. He concluded that Aunt Maggie couldn't be sure that he, Ben, would be the one who opened the letter. So she must have been intentionally vague, to give a potential stranger as little information as possible. Yeah, that seemed plausible.

Next, he thought that Maggie *must* have known that the Strat was valuable. After all, she was in the music biz, not stuck behind a desk the way Ben had been for the last three decades. And if the Strat was worth a lot of money, *imagine* how valuable Red's guitar must be!

OK, he wasn't sure if those were all logical conclusions…but it gave him something to sleep on.

***

He picked up the Strat, cradling it more carefully than he had earlier, and headed back to his parents' house for dinner, hoping his mother was able to find his old Gibson catalog. The one with the green trees on the cover. He wanted to see the picture of the Melody Maker that Angie referred to as "version four."

***

When he walked through the door, his dad said, "Hey, I found a picture of Maggie's singing group." He handed Ben a faded 8x10 promo picture.

It was a typical promotional photo from the 1950s. Black and white. A cheesy photography studio shot, with a corny prop. Three guys and a girl leaning on a ladder. The guys were in suits, and the girl, Maggie, wore a mid-length white dress. There were no instruments in the picture, which would explain his dad's conclusion that they were a just singing group.

Ben casually turned it over.

Hand-written on the back, in faded pencil, were the names of the band members: *Maggie May, Bill "Sticks" Barton, Randy Roberts, and Bob "Mr. Bassman" Stewart.*

Chapter Four

"Hello, may I speak to Bob Stewart please?"

Ben may not have been a vintage guitar expert, but he was very talented at finding solutions. In his job at Bismark Insurance he had spent the last thirty years solving problems. Other than the musicians' individual names, Aunt Maggie's promo photo didn't offer any clues; there was no band name, booking agent, or phone numbers. But Ben wouldn't give up that easily.

Over dinner with his parents he started asking questions. His father told him that Maggie had left town at the age of eighteen and rarely returned. "She spent all of her time traveling with that singing group," his dad said, "I think she adopted them as a backup family."

If Maggie and the band were that close, Ben reasoned, they probably kept in touch. And perhaps the band members heard that she passed away. And Bob Stewart may have sent flowers or a card.

Since Ben's father was Maggie's eldest sibling, and she had never married, he asked his dad if the funeral paperwork and sympathy cards had been forwarded to him. They had. During their post-dinner tea, Ben and his parents sifted through the papers. It didn't take long to find it: a sympathy card from Mr. & Mrs. Bob Stewart, with a return address in Ford City, PA. Ben logged onto the internet with his iPhone and in a minute had the Stewarts' phone number.

The next morning he called.

**

"Who's calling?" an elderly woman's voice asked.

"Hi, this is Ben Cooper, Maggie Cooper's nephew. I inherited Maggie's guitar, and I have a question about it for Mr. Stewart."

"Oh, hi, Ben! This is Mary Stewart. Bob will be happy to hear from you. You know, Maggie always said she was going to leave that guitar to you."

He was a little unnerved by the comment. He barely knew his aunt, let alone Bob and Mary Stewart, but they all seemed to know him!

"Well, I'm very happy to have the guitar. Is your husband around?"

"No, no, he's down the road at St. Mark's Personal Care Home. His arthritis got so bad lately that it was hard for me to take care of him. He's been there for a few months and really likes it. I visit him every day."

"Oh, ah... I see..." Ben didn't know what to say.

"As long as you're coming up to talk to him," Mary continued, "Maybe you could buy his bass. Bob can't play it anymore and I don't want to put an ad in the paper. I don't want strangers coming over."

"Oh... I wasn't planning on driving there...but I guess I could," Ben stammered.

"Good. Good. You're like family. I know you'll give me a fair price on the bass."

"Yeah, sure," Ben said. "What kind of bass is it?"

"You know," Mary said. "The kind with four strings. I'm sure it's worth a lot of money. It's really old, just like me and Bob!"

She continued, "How about noon tomorrow? Pick me up and we'll go visit him."

"OK, thanks," he said as he slowly hung up the phone. He had only wanted to ask Bob about "Red," the person in Maggie's cryptic letter. Now he was apparently buying a bass. He appreciated the fact that Mary trusted him enough to give her a "fair" price... and he wanted to. He liked Mary immediately. And even though these folks were complete strangers, Ben's dad was right, they already kind of felt like family.

He stood there for a second, pondering his next move. He was going to need help. He called the office and told them he'd be late. Grabbing his car keys, he headed out the door. It was time for his third trip in two days to Pittsburgh Guitars.

***

"Hey! Back again!" said Sam. "I don't think your Melody Maker is ready yet…"

"No, no, it's not that," said Ben. "I'm going to look at a vintage bass tomorrow. But I won't know what to pay for it."

"Well," said Sam, "There's tons of info on the internet. Or you could call us here when you have it in front of you…"

Looking up at all of the sizes and shapes of guitars hanging around the store, Ben said, "But I have to at least know what I'm describing in order to describe it. My problem is that I don't know what I don't know."

"Ah," said Sam, "the story of life."

"Could you get away for a few hours tomorrow, to help me?" Ben said. "It's about an hour drive."

"Sorry, man, I've gotta work," said Sam.

Then, after a quick thought, Sam continued, "But hey, you know who could help? Remember that girl you were talking to outside, yesterday morning? Angie?"

Ben acted nonchalant. But, yes, of course he remembered her.

"She could give you some buying advice."

Pretending to be slightly intrigued, but actually *very* intrigued, Ben asked, "What's her story anyway?"

"I'm not sure," said Sam. "She first started coming in here in 2006, right in the thick of the vintage bubble. She had some expensive guitars she wanted us to help her sell."

"The vintage bubble?" asked Ben.

23

"Yeah, 2005 through 2007 or so."

He could see that Ben was interested. "Wanna hear the story?" he asked.

"Of course!" said Ben, smiling.

Sam sat back on the stool behind the counter.

"When we first started this store we sold used guitars. Then, in the 1980s, *used* guitars became *vintage* guitars." He put up his fingers to make hand air quotes around *used* and *vintage*.

"There were two main reasons. First of all, older guitars were simply better than new guitars made in the 80s and 90s. And second, the baby boomer guitar players started making enough money that they could afford to buy the guitars they had as kids... or the guitars they *wished* they had as kids."

Ben was following along so far...

Sam continued, "As more and more players looked for better and cooler vintage guitars, the demand increased. And of course, the supply is finite. You can't go back in time and make more. So prices steadily climbed."

"By the early 2000s," Sam said, "thanks to baby boomer guitarists having even more disposable income, prices began to get *so* high that guitars started to look like *investments*."

He used bigger air quotes on *investments*.

"That brought all sorts of new people into the market. People who were buying guitars primarily as investments, not to play them. This eventually happens with any collectible field. People buying and selling things back and forth for higher and higher prices, all based on perceived future return value. The sad thing is that this drives actual players, the people who wanted the guitars in the first place, out of the market."

Ben understood. He said, "So then prices spiraled upward until everything crashed."

"Exactly," said Sam.

"What now?" Ben asked.

"In recent years prices have settled down to what they normally would have risen to. In other words, they're still up from pre-bubble prices. In the long run they've always gone up. They're just down from the artificial bubble high prices."

"And what about you guys?" Ben asked.

Sam smiled. "Well, with regard to our personal collections, we love our guitars too much to sell them. Maybe we *should* have sold everything at the height of the bubble… But we'd still rather have the guitars! With regard to the store, we've been around for long enough that we knew not to get too caught up in all of that. We didn't over-pay for too many things during the bubble, so we're good."

"And Angie…." said Ben.

"Oh, right, getting back to her," said Sam, "When we first met her, she had a lot of guitars. And she sold them when the selling was good. We helped with some high dollar ones, but then she started handling it herself. She knows her stuff."

"Sounds like she'd be a big help tomorrow. Can you give me her number?"

"No." said Sam, "But we have your number on your repair receipt. How 'bout I pass that on to her?"

"That would be great, Sam," said Ben. "And thanks for the story. I learn something new every time I stop here."

***

Ben had planned to head into the office, for a half-day. But after his visit to the guitar store he decided to take the rest of the day off. Then he took another vacation day for his visit to Bob and Mary Stewart tomorrow. He was enjoying this new found freedom…and the excitement of learning about vintage guitars. He was especially looking forward to discovering all of those things that he didn't know he didn't know.

***

Two hours later his phone rang. It was Angie.

"I hear we're going on a road trip!"

Chapter Five

A car horn beeped twice. Angie was five minutes early.

Ben's conversation with her the night before was brief. He had explained that he needed to go to Ford City, an hour away, to buy an old bass; and he was looking for expert guidance. She said, "No problem. I'll drive."

It had already been a busy morning. Angie's only advice during the evening phone call was that he bring "a couple of thousand" in cash, so he went to his bank as soon as they opened. Ben had certainly made large purchases before, after all he owned a car and a house, but those were all paid by check. He was a little uncomfortable with the large envelope of twenties that he carried out of the bank.

Back at his place, he spent the next hour playing the `56 Strat he had inherited from his Aunt Maggie. He loved the way the guitar felt, especially the back of the neck, where the finish had been worn off by years of use. The bare wood made it very comfortable, and fast, to play chords up and down the neck. He even experimented with a few solos. Not bad, he thought. It reminded him of the fun he had playing with his band back in the 1980s.

But something was different now. In his teens his goal was to be 'rich and famous.' And that goal was tied to the guitar. The amount of pleasure he got from playing the instrument was inevitably attached to how close, or far, he felt from that goal.

Now, in his late 50s, sitting in his living room, waiting for Angie's arrival, there was no chance of him becoming a rich and famous rock star. With that goal removed, he found that he was truly enjoying himself.

There was no pressure, just the peaceful joy of creating music. "Playing guitar is fun," he smiled to himself.

***

The car horn startled him, and he quickly put away the Strat, grabbed his coat, and headed out the door.

"Good to see ya," he said, as he hurriedly got in the car.

Yesterday's activities had been a blur. Visiting a guitar store instead of going to work, carrying a potentially vintage and expensive gift from a late aunt, and running into a stranger on the street who listed dates and guitar models as fast as she could speak was a lot to take in. This morning, getting into the car of a relative stranger, with $2,000 in his pocket, and a vague plan to meet an aging bass player, he was again out of his element. Life had taken an odd turn.

Today Angie's dark brown hair fell to her shoulders rather than staying hidden up under the wool cap she had worn at Pittsburgh Guitars. He liked it. And as she turned toward him he could see a sparkle in her eyes. An enthusiasm for life. Some people have it, most don't.

"Sorry if I rushed you." said Angie. "My philosophy is 'if you're not five minutes early, you're late'," she laughed.

"No problem," said Ben. "Here's the address for your GPS."

Angie's car was a brand new white Subaru. That, combined with the fact that she had no problem making last minute plans in the middle of the workweek, made Ben curious about what she did for a living. But it was too early to ask.

"Thanks for letting me drive," she said as they pulled away from the curb. "Sam at the guitar store said you were okay, and I didn't find anything online that suggested you were an ax-murderer, but I still figured it would be better if I had control of the passenger ejector seat."

He assumed she was kidding, but he looked around the car just the same.

"Here, I brought you a present." She reached beside her seat and handed him a manila envelope.

Ben opened it, and smiled. A 1966 Gibson guitar catalog, just like the one his guitar teacher Victor Lawrence had given him when his mother bought the Melody Maker all those years ago. And just like the one he and Angie talked about two days ago.

"Thank you so much!" he said. "I wasn't able to find mine."

"It's a gift. I have three or four copies. I told you it was the most common old Gibson catalog. The Melody Makers are on page 11."

He turned to page 11, and there, just as he remembered, was a "Melody Maker." And it looked nothing like his.

"This is version four," Ben said, proud that he could remember the model differences she originally described to him.

"Yeah, they kept changing the body shape on that guitar. Same electronics, though. And same skinny headstock," she said.

As he read the description in the catalog, Angie continued without taking her eyes off the road.

"There's one thing that's not in any catalog, though. And this'll be good if you're ever in a bar bet over Gibson guitar models."

Ben laughed, trying to imagine himself placing bets over Gibson guitars.

She continued, "Most people don't know this, but they actually made a twelve string version of that Melody Maker. And they only made a couple hundred of them, compared to the almost 50,000 Melody Makers out there. So those are really rare."

"And they only did that with version four?" Ben asked.

"Yep. So if you ever see one, it's rare."

"Is it worth a lot of money?"

29

"Well, rare doesn't always mean valuable, but it is worth a little more than the other version fours…"

"There sure is a lot to learn about old guitars," Ben said.

"I suppose," said Angie. "But it's fun to learn about things that interest you."

She's right about that, he thought. Sometimes he dreaded learning the details of new projects at work, but now he couldn't get enough about guitars. Especially coming from Angie.

"How do you know so much about guitars? What got you started?" he asked.

"Oh, it's a long story…"

"We've got an hour," he said.

"It all goes back to a guy," she said, still staring at the road.

He wondered if he had strayed too far into personal territory. He considered changing the topic. She hesitated slightly, but then continued.

"It was back in the 1990s," she said. "I was dating a musician. Rick, a guitar player."

She seemed to smile at the thought. Ben was relieved.

"His band was pretty good. And the relationship was okay, initially. But Rick was *very* into his guitar. A 335."

Glancing at Ben she added more detail, "It was a Gibson ES-335. A thin semi-hollow body. And it was all he talked about. Every time we saw a musician on TV or in a magazine, he'd point out 335s. He'd say, 'Look, there's Eric Clapton with a 335!' or 'Look, there's B.B. King with a 335!' or 'Look, there's Chuck Berry with a 335!' At first it was cute. Then it got annoying." She laughed.

"The truth is, he was happier with that guitar than he was with me. I think it was his real love. He spent so much time playing with his band, that that guitar became the center of his world.

"Eventually I got frustrated, and started to question him and the entire relationship. And I started to question that damn 335. I saw it every day. I knew it well."

"I think I know the guitar you're talking about," said Ben. "I've seen B. B. King."

"Good. Well, one day I ran across a picture of B.B. King in *Rolling Stone*, and I thought, 'There's something odd about his 335.' I noticed that the headstock on his guitar was fancier than Rick's guitar. When I looked closer, there were other differences, too.

"That made me curious, so I searched around for a picture of Chuck Berry. His headstock matched Rick's, but the fingerboard inlays were different.

"At that point I was so disheartened with my relationship with Rick that I decided to figure out what was wrong with his 335. Almost out of spite, I guess."

"And *was* something wrong?" Ben asked, fascinated by the story.

"Well, this was before everything in the world was on the internet, and there weren't many books about guitars back then. But I found one called *American Guitars* by Tom Wheeler. It's a great book. I still have it.

"Anyway, it turned out..." She looked over at him, "As I'm sure you know..."

"No, I don't!" said Ben quickly.

"It turned out," she continued, now looking back at the road, "that there are three different models, a 335, 345 and 355. Rick's 335 is the plain one. The 345 is a little fancier, with split parallelogram inlays, a Varitone switch, and gold hardware. And the 355 is the fanciest. It's like a Les Paul Custom version of the 335, with a bound headstock, ebony fingerboard with block inlays, multiple layers of binding around the body, and gold hardware...plus the Varitone switch."

She was throwing out a lot of details, and he had no idea what a Varitone switch was. But he nodded, trying to take it all in.

"I finally dumped Rick, but I kept the book. And the more I read about guitars, the more I enjoyed it. I didn't play at the time, but I seemed to be pretty adept at remembering guitar models. It just came easy to me."

"And that got you started with guitars?" asked Ben.

"Yeah. To help deal with the break-up, I bought myself a 345. It was ten better than his," she laughed, "you know, a 345 versus a 335!"

Ben smiled at the inside joke. One that he wouldn't have understood ten minutes earlier.

"Six months later, I sold it. For more than I paid for it! So then I used that money to buy a 355. *Twenty* better! Ha!"

Angie was smiling back at Ben now.

"Looking back, that era was pretty interesting. In those days nobody really knew what they had. If you did some research, and knew what you were buying, you could make a lot of money.

"Without planning to do it, I ended up buying and selling a lot of guitars. Eventually, I started to hang on to the ones that I thought were the best investments.

"By 2005 I had quite a collection."

"What happened then?" Ben asked.

"Well, I've never been the kind of person who gets attached to stuff…"

Chapter Six

As Angie opened up about her life, Ben pondered his.

He wasn't thrilled about the prospect of another birthday next month. But one advantage of his increasing age was the ability to look back at his youth more objectively. His early-20s attempt to be a rock star had proved fruitless. Now, though, he understood that his band did not have either of the two key things needed to make it big in show biz: spectacular talent, or unique weirdness. We were good, he thought, but not special.

He was at peace with it. The band had been fun, and his onstage experience proved helpful when he entered the business world, where he was at ease giving presentations and leading group meetings. When his thoughts turned to his job, though, he faced a bit of an internal struggle, as he attempted to convince himself that those were decades well spent. His position in the company and his bank statement seemed to indicate a successful career. But for as long as he could remember, his life had been the same consistent and boring routine.

All of that changed this week with the arrival of Aunt Maggie's guitar.

***

As he listened to Angie describe the guitars she had purchased over the years he found himself fascinated with every aspect of the vintage guitar world. Who started these companies? How many models did each company make? How did the different models change over the years? And why? After years of tedious work in the business world, he suddenly found himself getting passionate about something.

Oddly though, he didn't sense that emotion in Angie's voice. True, she was an expert in the details. And he loved listening to her talk about old guitars. But as she rattled off brands and model designations, he wondered if they were just numbers to her.

She continued, "In 2006 and 2007, guitar prices got out of hand. Too many people were paying super-high prices just based on speculation. Even the dealers were selling stuff back and forth between themselves, always at higher prices.

"I decided it was time to cash out, so I did. Timing a price bubble is a difficult thing to do. But I was watching the market closely.

"To be honest, things didn't collapse as much as I expected. Prices certainly dropped in 2008, enough to scare some folks, especially the ones who had paid top-dollar prices in 2006. But things mostly bounced back. Prices are pretty high right now.

"Anyway, I held on to a few, but I sold most of my guitars back then. Some of them were for big bucks. It worked out well."

That might explain her apparent lack of a job, Ben thought.

He wanted to ask her if she felt any personal attachment to any of these guitars, but just then they turned on to Main Street in Ford City.

Angie laughed and said, "Main Street, every town's got one."

"And look," Ben noted, "It's also Route 66!"

"Then I guess this is where we should start, 'when we plan to motor west...'" she said.

He was impressed that she knew the first line of the song *Route 66*. He wondered if she knew as much about music as she did about guitars. Back in his younger days he'd shop at Jim's Records every Saturday, carrying home a stack of vinyl. He made a mental note to dig out his old LPs when he got home.

They passed the five or six blocks of "downtown" Ford City rather quickly, and soon found themselves among typical 1950s suburban houses, much like the one he grew up in. The Stewart house was easy to find. Especially since there was a carved wooden musical note on the mailbox at the end of the driveway.

They parked and got out of the car, but before they reached the front door, Angie grabbed his arm and turned him back toward the car.

"I forgot to ask," she said, "Am I 'good cop' or 'bad cop'?"

"What?" Ben asked, totally confused by the question.

"You know," she whispered, "When we see the bass, one of us will be all enthusiastic about it and friendly, and the other one will be totally against it. It'll give us more negotiating leverage." "No, no," said Ben. "We're here to buy the bass, no matter what. You just tell me what it's worth."

By the time they reached the porch, Mary Stewart was in the doorway.

"Benjamin! So nice to finally meet you," she said. "Come on in!"

Reaching to shake Angie's hand, she said, "And are you Benjamin's wife?"

"Oh, no!" said Angie, surprised. Quickly recovering, Angie added, "Just a friend."

"This is Angie, Mrs. Stewart," said Ben. "And thank you so much for taking us to see Bob today."

"Oh, he'll be glad to see you. He spent so many years traveling with your Aunt Maggie. They were like brother and sister. He'd be happy to help you out. And, please, call me Mary."

Ben noticed the ragged, oddly shaped case leaning against the couch.

"And is that Bob's bass?"

"Yes. Yes, it is," she said. "You look it over. I'll make us some tea. Would you like a sandwich?"

"No thanks, Mary," Ben said with a smile as she walked out of the room.

35

Turning toward the case, Ben said to Angie, "Would you like to do the honors?"

"No," she replied, "If you're going to start buying guitars, you may as well start now."

Ben gently put the case on the couch. The back hinges were loose, and the top of the case barely stayed attached as he opened it.

He was immediately glad that Angie was nearby. He had no idea what he was looking at. It was violin-shaped, like the bass that Paul McCartney plays. Hofner, he thought? Yeah, Paul's is a Hofner. But this was solid brown, not the sunburst color of Paul's bass. The pickguard and the pickup were also brown. And there was a small black f-hole painted on the front and a thin black pin-stripe around the edge. It was unlike anything he had ever seen before. He wondered if this was some sort of odd Hofner copy. But as his eyes followed the strings up the neck to the headstock, he saw that it said 'Gibson.'

He carefully picked it up. It was heavier than he expected. At first it looked like the tuner buttons were broken off, but then he noticed that they stuck out from the back.

"It's an EB-1," said Angie, still standing across the room.

"Wow," said Ben, impressed at both the oddness of the bass and the quickness of her assessment.

He was further surprised by her next comment, "How bad is the headstock crack?"

"How do you know it's…" He didn't even have time to finish his question, as he turned the bass around and looked at the back of the headstock. Sure enough, there was a faint, but definite, u-shaped crack. Angie continually amazed him.

"How did you know?" he asked.

"Those machine heads are known as 'banjo tuners' since they're like the ones used on banjos. I don't know why Gibson ever used them, 'cause

36

they're the first point of contact with even the slightest drop. And the headstock rests on those tuners in the case. So even in the case it isn't safe. Most guitars with banjo tuners end up with cracked headstocks.

"What year is it?" she asked.

Ben looked again at the back of the headstock. The serial number was stamped on in black ink.

"It says 4, and then a space, and then 0231."

"That's cool," she said. "That makes it a 1954, the second year for that bass."

"Do you have all of the numbers memorized?" he asked, wondering if that was even possible.

"Solid-bodies in the 1950s are easy," Angie said, as she walked toward him and held out her hand for the bass.

As she looked it over, she continued, "In the `50s the first digit was the year. In this case, the 4 means 1954."

Then she looked back up and pointed at him to emphasize her words, "That's *only* true of inked-on serial numbers on Gibson solid-bodies in the 50s."

He smiled. It was as if she was some kind of cute, yet strict, teacher, who wanted him to get things right, right from the beginning.

"What do you think it's worth?" he asked.

"You know what's interesting…" she said, ignoring his question. He could tell that her brain was processing information faster than his. "You said that when you asked Bob's wife what model this was, she just called it a 'bass.' Well, she was right. When this was introduced, and probably when Bob bought it, the official model name was the 'Electric Bass.' Gibson retroactively re-named it the EB-1 in 1958 when they introduced their second bass, the hollow-body EB-2."

Looking down at the bass in her lap, she slowly moved her hand across its contoured top.

"So, now this is known as an EB-1. But from 1953 until 1958 it was just the 'Electric Bass.'"

"Why would they use such a generic name?" Ben asked.

"It could have been lack of imagination. But my guess is ego." Angie replied. "Fender's Precision Bass came out a year earlier, in 1952, and people were already referring to the Fender bass just as the 'electric bass'. In fact, all through the 1950s, if you said 'electric bass' people knew you meant a Fender P-Bass. Gibson was probably trying to pre-empt that by calling *their* bass the quote *Electric Bass* unquote. But it never caught on."

"The name?" he asked.

"The name and the bass," said Angie. "In the six years that they made this bass, the EB-1 or Electric Bass, or whatever you want to call it, average sales were less than 100 a year."

"So it's pretty rare?" Ben asked. "Is it a bad bass?"

"It's very well made, just like a Les Paul," she said. "But the problem with the bass, both then and now, is that it's very boomy." She pointed to the wide, brown plastic-covered pickup. "With just this one pickup, positioned up near the end of the fingerboard, you get a *lot* of low end. Too much low end for the amps made in the 50s. So, when this bass was made, there weren't any amps that could handle it. At least not at any kind of volume."

"What should I pay for it?" Ben asked.

They could hear tea cups rattling as Mary Stewart returned from the kitchen.

Angie whispered to Ben, "Should we go outside and talk about it?"

Ben whispered back to her, "No, we can talk about it in front of Mary..."

Angie looked at him with a stern look on her face, still whispering, "Alright. But next time we're doing this my way."

Next time? Ben liked the sound of that.

Chapter Seven

"I don't know a lot about vintage instruments, so I brought Angie to help me," Ben said, as Mary Stewart placed tea cups on the coffee table in front of them.

"That's nice," she replied, handing Ben a cup of tea.

Looking at Angie, who was still holding the bass, she asked, "And what do you think, dear?"

Angie glanced over at Ben. He could see by the look on her face that she wanted to discuss the purchase with him in private. Smiling, he said, "Yes, what do you think, Angie?"

She didn't speak, but her expression changed to resignation, as if to say, "OK, if that's what you want."

She turned and looked back to Mary.

"In its current condition, but without the headstock crack, it's worth around $5,000." Turning the back of the bass toward Mary and pointing at the headstock crack, she said, "With the crack, I'd pay $3,000."

Looking back at Ben, she added, "It's going to be hard to re-sell with the crack…"

"Oh, I'm not going to re-sell it," Ben said, "I'm going to keep it with Aunt Maggie's Strat. It's not going to fall apart is it?"

"No," said Angie. "It looks like a decent repair. It's perfectly fine to play. But the crack heavily affects its market value."

She was frustrated that they were having this discussion in front of the seller.

Ben turned to Mary, and said, "I'd like to give you $5,000 for it."

40

Mary looked at him and smiled, Angie looked at him in confusion…
simultaneously they both said, "Really?"

"Unfortunately," he said, as he pulled an envelope from his pocket,
"I only brought $2,000 with me, so I'll have to come back…"

Angie sighed. Shaking her head in disbelief, she picked up her purse
from the couch, and opened it with the flap sticking up so that neither of
them could see what she was doing. He could hear her rustling with an
envelope in her purse, and then she handed him three neat stacks of $100
bills, still with the striped paper bank wrappers around them.

"Here. You can pay me back when we get home."

Ben rarely ran across a solitary $100 bill in his normal life, so seeing
$3,000 in hundreds was a bit of a shock.

He handed his large stack of twenty-dollar bills, and Angie's three
packs of hundreds to Mary.

"Oh, that's much more than I expected!" she said. "Thank you both
very much!" Without counting it she turned and placed the money in the
top drawer of an end table near the couch, and said, "Finish your tea, and
we'll go to see Bob!"

***

Ben helped Mary into the passenger seat of Angie's car and they
headed back out to Main Street. It would be a short trip. St. Mark's
Personal Care Home was only two miles away.

Angie asked, "Mary, how long have you and Bob been married?"

"Since 1960, dear," she replied. "We met a few years before that,
when his band was passing through town, and we kept in touch. In 1960
they took a break, and he came here to visit me. One thing led to another
and we got married. We had a wonderful time setting up the house! But
eventually he had to go back on the road. He'd come back whenever

possible, though. And a few times he brought Maggie. That's how I got to know her. She was always so nice.

"In the 1980s they all finally got tired of the traveling. They ended the band and Bob moved back for good. So the first 25 years were hit or miss, but we've been with each other every day since!"

"At least until a few weeks ago…" she added with a touch of sadness. Perking back up she said, "Well, we're *still* with each other every day! Here it is dear, turn right."

Angie pulled into the parking lot of the assisted living home. They got out of the car and Mary led them in to the reception area. She said, "Wait here, I'll see if he's ready."

Ben whispered to Angie, "I guess we all eventually end up in a place like this…"

"If we're lucky," Angie whispered back. "And, you know, you could have gotten that bass cheaper."

Ben smiled, and said, "Next time I'll let you do the negotiating. Thanks for the loan, by the way. What's up with all of the cash?"

"I was hoping it would be a stack-knob Jazz Bass…" she said.

"A what?" Ben asked. Then he saw Mary waving to them from down the hallway, motioning for them to join her. Ben and Angie walked down to Room 103 and entered. Sitting in a chair next to the bed was Bob "Mr. Bass Man" Stewart, the man mentioned in the note hidden in Aunt Maggie's guitar.

Ben reached over to shake his hand, and he could feel the arthritic stiffness in Bob's fingers. Ben resolved then and there that when he got home he was going to play his guitar every day, before his hands ended up like Bob's.

"It's nice to finally meet you, Ben. Mary tells me you gave her a lot of money for the bass. Thanks, I appreciate it."

"I'm happy to have it, Mr. Stewart," said Ben, "I'm going to keep it with Aunt Maggie's guitar."

"That's great. It's nice to know that even when the band is gone our instruments will still be together! Ha, I should give Bill's wife a call and see if she still has his drums!"

"I may take you up on that," Ben said. Remembering Angie standing right beside him, Ben said, "Oh, I'm sorry, this is Angie…"

"Your wife?" Bob asked, reaching up to shake her hand.

"No, just a friend," said Angie.

Ben and Angie moved to two small chairs in the corner of the room. Mary sat on the bed next to Bob, holding his hand.

"Tell me about Maggie," Ben asked.

"Well…" Bob said, gazing upward, trying to recall the correct year, "I think I met her in 1957.

"She was living in New York City, singing and playing guitar in small clubs. She was just strumming chords on an acoustic, but she had a voice like an angel. My band… me, Bill and Randy… Randy Roberts, on piano… we were working in the lounge at some hotel on Broadway. I forget which one, we've been to New York so many times. Anyway, we had a night off, and we stumbled into this little club where Maggie was singing. We all fell in love with her right away and invited her to see our group the next night.

"We also all tried to ask her out, but ha!, she was tough. I guess being a young girl in New York, you get your street smarts pretty quick.

"The next night she came to see our act. We asked her up to do a song, and it was like magic right away. Roger and I did a lot of nice vocals, but her voice added the missing ingredient in our harmonies. Even if she wouldn't date any of us, we all wanted her to join the band as soon as possible.

"The guitar was a nice touch, too."

"What kind of guitar was it?" Ben asked.

"It was a small Martin… a double O or triple O… I never knew the difference."

"The 00 is smaller than the 000," Angie interjected.

Bob and Ben looked at her. Bob continued, "Well, it was a cheap one, a 00 or 000-18."

Ben looked back at Angie. "And today?" he asked.

"$3,000 to $4,000" she said.

Ben and Bob both smiled. Getting back to the story, Bob said, "Well, she packed her stuff and left with us at the end of the week. And with her in the band we got a lot more work and made a lot more money. It was more fun, too!"

"So, she only played acoustic?" Ben asked.

"Originally, yes," Bob replied. "But we soon got one of those pickups that fit across the soundhole.

"At first we plugged her into my amp. I had a new Fender Bassman, which was pretty funny because folks had been calling me Bob 'Mr. Bassman' since I played upright in high school. I never cared much for how that amp sounded, though. Anyway, eventually we got her her own amp… I believe it was a Fender Deluxe.

"We worked non-stop in those days…all over New York, Pennsylvania, Ohio, Michigan. Maggie was with us when we first played here in town, wasn't she Mary?"

"Yes, dear," said Mary.

"What about the Stratocaster?" Ben asked.

"She got that in Pittsburgh," Bob answered. "She had to go home to help out with her dad… your grandfather. He had some sort of health scare, and she had to go home for a while. I think that was in '59?"

Mary corrected him, "It was 1960, dear. That's when we got married."

44

"Oh, yes!" Bob laughed. Looking at Mary he said, "It's been so wonderful I wanted to add a year." She smiled back at him.

He continued, "We took a break from the band for almost a year while Maggie was in Pittsburgh. When she came back she had the Strat, and she was a *much* better player. She must have practiced the entire time she was home!

"She only played the Strat from then on. At first she still used the Deluxe amp, but one night her amp was acting up and she plugged into my Bassman. And it sounded fabulous. We were in New York…again…and the Ampeg company had just introduced the B-15, that amp with a flip-top amp head. And it sounded *really* good with my bass. So I bought one, It was one of the first ones they made. Once I got the Ampeg, Maggie only used my Bassman."

Angie had been glancing around the room while listening to Bob. Suddenly something caught her eye. Leaning against Bob's dresser was a walking cane. Its handle was a carved duck head, but she thought she recognized the rest of it. She had to ask.

"I'm so sorry to interrupt," she said, leaning in towards Bob, and pointing at the cane. "Did you carve that duck head?" she asked.

"Yes, I did!" Bob said, happy to see someone appreciate his work.

"And is it screwed on to the extension rod from your Electric Bass?" she asked.

"Ah ha ha!" Bob laughed. "Where did you find her, Ben? Yes, yes, it is! I had completely forgotten about that!"

Ben was confused.

Seeing the look on his face, Angie explained, "Until the Fender Precision, all bass players played the upright bass. When Gibson introduced *their* bass, the one Bob had, they thought that people might still want to play it vertically, like an upright. So it came with an extendable rod that screwed into the bottom where the lower strap button

45

would be. In theory, you could play it straight up and down like an upright bass."

"In *theory*," Bob laughed.

Angie smiled at him and continued, "A real upright is big, and you can hold it steady against your body. The Gibson bass is shaped like a miniature upright, but it's so small that it spins around if you try to play it like an upright."

"It never did work," said Bob, "But it was okay as a cane. You kids take that, too. It goes with the bass, and I have other canes. You can keep the duck head as well!"

"Thanks Mr. Stewart!" said Ben.

"Now, tell me, what really brings you to Ford City?"

Chapter Eight

Dear Benjamin,
Please help Red with his guitar. It might be valuable.
Mr. Bassman will know where he is.
Love, Maggie
PS: I hope you like the Strat

Bob Stewart handed the letter back to Ben.

Glancing away in thought he said, almost to himself, "Red Brown...I haven't seen him in fifty years."

"Red Brown?" said Ben, holding back a smile at the unusual name.

Looking over at Ben, Bob laughed. "I hadn't thought about that in years, but, yeah, it is a funny name. I don't know what his real first name is. Everyone knew him as 'Red' because...well..." Bob pointed at his head. "His hair is probably white now."

"Did he play in the band?" Ben asked.

"No, no," said Bob. "He was a fan. I think he lived in Battle Creek. He used to come out to see us whenever we were booked there, or in Kalamazoo. I think he even came to Detroit once. He was really funny. And creative. He was always drawing sketches on bar napkins.

"Maggie really liked him. He'd be waiting for us when we came to town, and they'd spend a lot of time together. They used to talk on the phone a lot, too. I think he wanted her to settle down with him in Michigan. But she couldn't do it. She wanted to stay on the road with the band.

"Eventually he stopped coming around. In the late 50's I think. I never saw him again."

Ben listened intently.

Bob continued, "In later years, every so often when we were on a long drive someone in the band would mention his name. But whenever they did, Maggie would get very quiet, with a sad look on her face. You know, to be honest, I think he was the only man she ever loved."

"Did he play guitar?" asked Ben.

"No, he didn't," said Bob. "He was a designer. I think he said that he even designed a car or two. He liked to sit and watch Maggie when she played, but he didn't play any instrument."

Glancing down at the note that Maggie had hidden in her Strat, Ben said, "Then what does this note mean? Why did Aunt Maggie say you'd know where he is?"

Bob looked at him and smiled. "Because I do."

Bob continued, "Maggie and I stayed in touch all these years. Mary and I even visited her in Florida a couple of times. And the last time I talked to her…she called around six months ago…out of the blue she said she was going to go to see Red. It was quite a surprise, because she hadn't mentioned his name since the 60s. But she said she was making plans to go to Bethlehem to see him. Bethlehem, PA, of course. It's over near Allentown…"

Ben nodded. He had traveled to eastern Pennsylvania on business. He knew where Allentown and Bethlehem were.

"Do you think she ever made the trip?" he asked.

Bob shook his head. "I don't know. She wasn't feeling well at the time, but she really wanted to go. It seemed very important to her. I don't know if she ever went."

"Wow," said Ben, at a loss for words. Slightly taken aback by all of this information, he wondered what to do next. He presumed Bethlehem wasn't a very big city. But without knowing Red's first name, it would be hard to find him.

Even though he could guess the answer, he asked anyway, "And you don't know anything about a guitar that Red may have?"

"No, Ben. I'm sorry, I don't," said Bob.

Throwing out an idea, to no one in particular, Ben said, "I suppose I could look online for music stores near Bethlehem and call them to ask about him. That would be easier than calling everyone in town named Brown."

Looking back at Bob, Ben said, "Can you remember anything else about him?"

"Well…" said Bob, trying to remember details from a half-century ago. "He was always drawing things. Machines, cars… oh, and trains! He would sketch trains."

Mary stood up. "Ben, Angie, would you like to join us for lunch?"

Ben could sense that they were wearing Bob out. And he was a little worried about the bass hidden in the hatchback of Angie's car.

"We have to head back," he said, "But thank you very much for everything."

"Yes, it was very nice meeting both of you," said Angie as she shook hands with Mary and Bob.

"Don't forget the cane," said Bob, pointing to his cane next to the bed.

Angie smiled, as she picked up the extension rod for the Electric Bass, with its added carved wooden duck head. "We won't!"

As Mary helped Bob up out of the chair, Ben had one more question, "I forgot to ask, what was the name of your group?"

"Oh, that changed over the years," Bob said. "It was originally The Randy Roberts Trio. When Maggie joined we changed it to The Randy Roberts Quartet for a while. But Maggie quickly became the star, so we decided to get her name out front. She didn't want to use her real last name… Cooper… like yours, right?"

"Yep, Ben Cooper," said Ben.

Bob continued, "So she used my name. We called it The Maggie Stewart Quartet. Then in the 60s we changed it to The Maggie Stewart Band, since that's what folks were calling us anyway."

"Do you mind if I come back someday and talk to you more about it?" Ben asked.

"Of course not," said Bob, "It was a lot of years on the road, but I wouldn't change any of it. After all, that's how I met Mary."

Bob and Mary smiled at each other. Ben could tell they were still very much in love.

"You kids go. I'm going to stay here a while," said Mary.

Bob reached out to shake hands with Ben. "Call or stop by anytime," he said.

***

Ben and Angie were both silent for the first fifteen minutes of the drive back to Pittsburgh.

Ben's new challenge was to find Red. He now knew his last name and where he lived. At least he had the city… Bethlehem, PA. But everything else was still a mystery. He wondered what kind of online searches would lead him to Red. And he was intrigued by the phone call that Maggie made to Bob. Did she ever make the trip to visit Red?

As they drove down Route 28, Ben looked over at Angie. She too seemed lost in thought.

"Thanks for your help with the bass," he said.

"You're welcome. It was fun," she replied.

Then she added, "I've been thinking about what he said, that his bass and Maggie's guitar will be together, even if they won't. It's funny, we

50

think we have so much control over our lives and all of the material things we own… but ultimately, the material stuff outlasts us."

"Not if it's technology, like computers or cell phones. Those things get thrown out every couple of years," Ben said.

"Yeah, okay, you got me there," she said, still in a thoughtful tone. "I was thinking more about guitars. I remember once when I was at a guitar show selling a 1913 Gibson L-1 to a guy, and we were talking about how old it was. And he said, 'You know, everyone originally associated with this guitar is dead. The guy who cut down the tree for the wood, the guy who built it, the guy at the factory who took the order, the guy who packed it up, the UPS guy who delivered it, and the original owner… all dead!' I just gave him a smart answer, and said, 'They didn't have UPS in 1913. But if they did, I bet the horse was brown.'"

She continued, "I didn't spend any time thinking about it then. But he was right. And that's probably true of a lot of the guitars I've bought and sold over the years. Each guitar was sought out…in a store or ordered from a catalog…purchased, played and loved by someone. And then…"

"Then it was passed on to someone else. And *they* played it and loved it," Ben said. "And each owner put a little bit of their soul into the guitar. I felt a special connection to Aunt Maggie when I played her Strat. It's like there is a part of her in that guitar. And I think it's kind of romantic that Maggie's guitar and Bob's bass can still make music together."

"I guess I never thought of guitars as *romantic*," said Angie. "I started buying them to get back at an old boyfriend. And I *kept* buying and selling them for the money. Guitars have just been a business to me."

"Well, we've got to change that!" said Ben, smiling.

He thought about the bass in the back of the car. He really did think it was romantic. The entire story was romantic… Bob and Mary meeting all those years ago, now growing old together and still holding hands. Bob and Maggie playing in a band for decades, maybe not "in love" but they certainly loved each other, she even used his last name. And, of course, Maggie and Red.

Yes, Red. He had to get back to that puzzle.

"You know," Angie said, interrupting his train of thought, "I don't think it's a good idea to call music stores near Bethlehem and ask if they know an old man who has a valuable guitar…"

"Good point," Ben said.

Then he suddenly remembered something he saw on TV last month. He loved to watch *CBS Sunday Morning*, a weekly hour-and-a-half show with eight or ten totally unrelated segments, on any imaginable topic, and always interesting. He loved the show because he never knew what he would see next, and he learned something new every week. Last month there was a segment about model trains. And most of the people they interviewed, including the main person in the story, were elderly men.

"Do you know anything about model train sets?" he asked Angie.

"I've seen a few when buying guitars," she said. "When you go to old folk's houses sometimes they want to show you their other collections. I remember a couple of old guys had pretty elaborate train setups. Why do you ask?"

"Bob told us that Red used to sketch trains in the old days," Ben said. "Maybe he's into model trains now." Ben was proud of his Sherlock Holmes approach to the situation. "Instead of calling guitar stores, maybe I can call hobby shops, and ask if they know anyone named Red?"

"Pretty clever," said Angie, impressed with his reasoning.

"But, you know what?" she added, "Bethlehem isn't far from Nazareth, where they make Martin guitars. They give free factory tours, and I have a really old Martin I wanted to show them anyway. Why don't we just drive there, take the Martin tour, and then go over to Bethlehem and ask around in person?"

"That would be great!" Ben said, shocked at the idea. It was a long drive across the state, but what an adventure!

"Can we go this weekend?"

"Okay," said Angie. "It will give us a chance to chat some more."

"You can tell me more about old guitars, and how valuable they are," said Ben.

"Sure," said Angie, "And you can tell me how romantic they are."

Chapter Nine

Friday morning. Back at the office.

Ben had a few meetings scheduled, but he wasn't looking forward to them. His mind was racing ahead to other plans. At lunch he was going to stop at his bank to withdraw the $3,000 he owed Angie. He also planned to dip into his savings account for another few thousand, in case he was able to find Red Brown and Red wanted to sell his guitar.

He had no idea what Red's guitar was or what it would be worth, but at least he knew from the trip to Ford City that he should take one-hundred-dollar bills and not twenties. The only question was how many hundreds he could carry around without feeling too nervous. He didn't know how much money Angie had with her at the Stewart house, but she had handed him the $3,000 as if it were $30. He decided that if *she* could be casual about it, he could too. He would walk out of the bank as calmly as any other day, no matter how many hundreds were in his pocket. It's all in the attitude, he told himself.

Right now, though, there were more pressing issues. Namely, the Ohio Project. His company was absorbing an Ohio insurance group and he was overseeing a group of project managers, as they prepared to merge the Ohio group's data systems with theirs. This was Ben's 35th year with Bismark Insurance, and the frustration level had never been higher. There were annoyed bosses above him, and stressed managers beneath him. And the sad thing was that no matter how hard he worked, he was ultimately at the mercy of those two groups. The tension was constant.

He focused on the computer screen in front of him. It contained yet another spreadsheet to analyze. When he heard his cell phone ring he was happy for the distraction. And even happier when he saw that it was Angie's number.

"Hello?"

"Hey Ben. Sorry to bother you at work," she said.

"No. No. Please, anytime."

"Yesterday we talked about going to Bethlehem and Nazareth this weekend," she continued, "but I can't get a Martin Factory Tour set up until next Thursday. I figure we can leave on Wednesday, be there for the morning tour on Thursday, and then look for your friend that afternoon. Can you get a few days off at the end of next week?"

"Absolutely," said Ben. "And if I can't get the days off, I'll quit."

"Ha! I'll leave that one up to you," said Angie. "I'll get us a couple of hotel rooms. Talk to ya next week."

"But, what about this money I owe you?" Ben asked.

"You can give it to me on Wednesday. Maybe we'll buy something on the way. See ya!"

"OK, great. I'll call you on Tuesday," said Ben, amazed at the difference between a conversation with Angie and the aggravating conversations he dealt with around the office. He thought he was joking when he told Angie that he'd quit if he couldn't get any days off. Now he wondered. Maybe his subconscious was trying to tell him something.

***

That night Ben spent some time playing the Gibson EB-1 bass. And then the Strat. He noticed that even without an amp, the Strat had a bright, ringing tone. Not very loud, but still fun to play. The bass, though, with its heavy flat-wound strings, made almost no noise at all. He clearly needed an amp. Or two. He decided to look around at Pittsburgh Guitars when he went to pick up his Melody Maker.

He leaned the bass against the couch, right next to the Strat. They weren't the most colorful instruments in the world, an all-brown bass and a brown sunburst guitar, but they had a definite magic to them. Ben tried to envision the thousands of miles those instruments traveled, and the thousands of songs they played together.

He thought it would be nice to have an on-stage photo of the Maggie Stewart Band. Perhaps he'd call Bob and Mary Stewart over the weekend, to ask if they had an "action" photo. In fact, he would need two copies of the picture. He'd keep one in each case, so future generations would know that these instruments belonged together.

***

The following morning over coffee he re-read the 1966 Gibson catalog that Angie gave him at the start of the Ford City trip.

He remembered that his bass was originally called the Electric Bass, but was re-named the EB-1 when a second bass was introduced. He turned to the bass section of the catalog. He couldn't find his bass there. He stopped for a second to try to recall everything Angie said. There were so many details. But he seemed to remember her saying something about six years. Yes, that was it. His bass was only made for six years. So it would have been discontinued long before the 1966 catalog.

He did find the second bass, though, the EB-2. As he compared it to other pictures in the catalog, he could see that the EB-2 was the bass version of the ES-335 guitar. The ES-335 was the guitar that Angie's ex-boyfriend played.

Next to the 335 in the catalog were the other models she mentioned, the ES-345 and the ES-355. And they were all gorgeous. He wondered what it would cost to own one of each. Sure, that might seem excessive, but it would be easy enough to store a few guitars in his spare bedroom.

And it would certainly be more practical than collecting something big...
like cars.

He flipped back to the bass section. Next to the EB-2 was another
bass, a red solid body, labeled the EB-3. That made sense. That must have
been Gibson's third bass. But the next photo surprised him. It was yet
another solid body bass, just like the EB-3, but the spelling of its name
was confusing. Directly under the photo it read EB-O, with the final
"letter" typeset as an "O." But in the descriptive paragraph beneath the
picture, the type said EB-0, with a zero. Both options seemed odd. EB-1,
EB-2, EB-3, then EB-O didn't make any sense. But EB-Zero sounded too
weird to be right.

Perhaps Angie could explain. Perhaps? Of course she could. He
wondered if he should start taking notes.

***

Saturday evening Ben went to his parent's house for dinner. Over his
mom's homemade meatloaf he talked about Bob and Mary, and how
happy they seemed together. He told them about how Bob's band met
Aunt Maggie in New York City. And how she joined the group. And all
of the many band names they used, eventually settling on Maggie's first
name and Bob's last name. His dad laughed at that.

He told them about Bob's bass, and Angie's help with its purchase.
Ben clearly admired Angie and smiled when he talked about her, which
made his parents happy. When Ben wasn't looking his mother gave a
subtle smiling nod to his dad. But they grew a bit concerned when he
started mentioning dollar figures. He spent $5,000 on a bass? And Angie
lent him more than half of it? They knew Ben had a good job, but they
never asked how much he made. Was it normal to spend that much on a
guitar? "No," Ben said, "Not in *normal* life." But *normal* life at Bismark
Insurance was wearing him out quickly.

Finally, as they were clearing the table, Ben said, "And I think Aunt Maggie's guitar might be from Pittsburgh."

"Oh, yeah?" said his dad.

"Well," said Ben, "Bob told me that Maggie only played acoustic until she came here to help Grandpa. And then when she returned to the band she only played the Strat."

"Help Grandpa?" his dad asked, "When was that?"

"1960. I remember because that's the year I was born. And Mary Stewart was sure of the year because that's when she and Bob got married."

"I remember when you were born, son. And your Aunt Maggie was nowhere around. She rarely came to visit in those days. I don't think we saw her that entire year."

"Grandpa didn't have some big health issue in 1960?" Ben asked.

"No, Ben. He was 81 when he passed away in 1975, and up until then your grandfather was never sick a day in his life."

Chapter Ten

"Hey Sam! It's me again."

7PM Monday night and Ben was back at Pittsburgh Guitars, this time carrying a ragged chipboard guitar case. There were three items on tonight's agenda: pickup his Melody Maker, drop off his Harmony Sovereign acoustic, and buy an amp or two.

Ben had spent Sunday playing the `56 Strat he inherited from Aunt Maggie. It didn't have much volume without an amp but when he held his ear against the guitar's body it sounded fantastic. He was surprised at how much he remembered from his days playing with the band over thirty years ago. He was a little rusty with the solos, but his fingers instinctively remembered the chords. The Strat inspired him to dig out his old acoustic, a Harmony Sovereign H1260. The Harmony had been stashed away in a basement closet for years, so he wasn't surprised to see that the strings were dark and corroded. They were also too high off of the fingerboard, making it difficult to play. It clearly needed some love and care.

***

"How did the Melody Maker turn out?" he asked Sam.

"It's in great shape," said Sam, "And it's nice to see one of these that's still 100% original."

"Is that unusual?" Ben asked.

"Well, this is probably one of the most modified models in the Gibson line," Sam replied. "These were meant to be beginners guitars, so they have pretty inexpensive pickups. But the over-all construction quality is just as good as Gibson's higher-priced guitars. Melody Makers have comfortable light-weight bodies and fabulous feeling necks. So, all you have to do is change the pickups, and maybe the machine heads, and you've got a pro instrument."

"Have you seen a lot of that?"

"Sure!" said Sam. "I guess the most famous is the white one Joan Jett plays."

"Hey, I remember seeing that." said Ben. "I have the album where she's jumping up in the air holding a white guitar. Is that a Melody Maker like mine?"

"It started out that way." replied Sam, "Joan bought it from Eric Carmen in The Raspberries. He had refinished it white and changed the pickups, so it already had two humbuckers before she got it. And since that album cover, she's done a *lot* more to it. Now it only has one pickup, a new pickguard, and tons of stickers."

"So is mine more valuable, since it's all original?" Ben asked.

"Well…" Sam replied, "Value has two sides to it. From an objective standpoint, if I had two vintage guitars in front of me and one was original and one was modified, then yes, the original one is much more valuable. But if you take the personal side into account, there are other ways to think of value. We have a customer who has an `81 Strat with a Kahler vibrato added. The Kahler requires a big cut in the guitar, so in a sense the value of that guitar has been ruined. But he's played a thousand gigs with it. It's been his main instrument for thirty years. And he wouldn't sell it for anything.

"Likewise, with Joan Jett. Her guitar is more valuable than yours because she's famous, of course. But even if you take fame out of the picture, I bet to *her* the guitar is priceless, just because it has been such a big part of her life."

"I see…" said Ben.

Sam continued, "If someone walked into the store today with a fifty-year-old vintage guitar and asked us to cut a hole in it, we wouldn't do it. If the guitar made it this far, we wouldn't devalue it now. But if someone came in with a fifty-year-old guitar that had been played and used and modified for decades, we wouldn't look down our noses at it. It's led a long, useful life, and it has its own value, to someone. I have a beat up, cracked, and dented Les Paul Special that's hardly worth anything marketwise, but I love it. I've played it all around the world. How could you put a price on that?

"Sorry to be longwinded. I'm just saying that value can be subjective."

"So," Ben said, "There is the market price, which is the general value… and the subjective price, if the guitar means something to you personally."

"Exactly," said Sam.

Ben understood completely. He had just overpaid, at least according to Angie, for Bob Stewart's bass. But the bass was extremely important to Ben. Certainly more important than the money.

He had tried to explain that to Angie in the car, but he didn't make much headway. Next time he'd use the Joan Jett story.

***

Sam wrote up a repair order for the Harmony acoustic, as Ben explained that he also needed a couple of amps, especially one for the newly purchased EB-1 bass. Sam demonstrated a sampling of amps around the store, and Ben settled on a small Vox guitar amp and a small Fender bass amp. Sam described them as "practice amps" since they were only 15 watts each. He said that the 15-watt guitar amp could be used in a gig situation, if the rest of the band wasn't too loud. But in Ben's case the bass amp would be better suited for home use.

"A bass as boomy as that EB-1 will easily overpower a small bass amp," Sam said. "If you want loud clean sound with that bass, you'll need some power behind you."

"Thanks, Sam," said Ben. "These two amps will do for now. I'm not ready for a public appearance yet. But who knows what the future will bring!" Ben laughed.

***

Back at home Ben checked the directions for the upcoming trip. He had GPS in his car, but sometimes he liked to print out directions as a backup. He also googled "Hobby Shops Bethlehem PA" and surprisingly found several. Very few of them seemed to have individual web sites, though, so he wondered if they'd even be in business when he and Angie arrived. He knew his idea to track down Red Brown through an interest in trains was a long shot. Especially since, as described by Bob, Red's train sketches were drawn more than 60 years ago. Plus, they were sketches of actual trains, not model trains. But Ben still felt it was a brainstorm of an idea.

And he was looking forward to the drive with Angie. He had to admit that the more time he spent with her, the more he liked her. She was a bit too analytical and numbers driven, especially numbers with dollar signs, but he sensed there was warmth in there somewhere. Besides, at work he was a numbers guy himself. After decades of studying spreadsheets, he could appreciate the decades of guitar identification details that Angie must have studied. The difference between them now was Ben's newfound excitement for a field that was old-hat to Angie.

***

Wednesday morning Angie pulled into Ben's driveway, five minutes early, just like last time. They decided to take her car again, although this

62

time they'd share the driving. The plan was to stay over in Nazareth, take the Thursday morning Martin factory tour, and then try to find Red Brown on Thursday afternoon.

As he was packing an overnight bag that morning, it occurred to Ben that they never really discussed what would happen beyond Thursday afternoon. If they didn't find Red, would they come straight home? If they did find him, would they stay over another night? He had been so preoccupied this week, jamming a dozen meetings into two work days, plus spending time with the guitar, bass and two new amps, that he didn't even think about anything beyond Thursday's search. And Angie never brought it up.

"Let's go find this guy!" she said, leaning on her car waiting for Ben.

"Okay," he said, throwing his bag in the backseat, "And I have lots of questions, both for you and Red."

As they turned right, and headed for the Pennsylvania Turnpike, Angie said, smiling, "What are the topics? Wait. Let me guess. Guitars?"

"For you," he replied, "question one: is it EB-Oh, or EB-zero? Question two: have you ever considered a guitar's value to be subjective? And are you familiar with Joan Jett? And question three: Have you ever wished you could go back and do it all over again?"

He wasn't sure where that last question came from. He had been thinking about Bob Stewart and how happy he was. Ben was in his late 50s and didn't exactly feel "old," not Bob-Stewart-old, but he wondered if he had made the most of his life so far. And then there was Sam, another example. Ben suspected he had more money in the bank than Sam did, but Sam sure seemed happier. Happy and free and enjoying his life. Ben wanted that feeling. He knew he couldn't go back in time. But he could still make changes in his future.

One thing was certain, last year at this time he would never had taken three days off, at the last minute, when a big project was in the works. He didn't know if it was the mysterious Red Brown quest, or Angie, or both, but his attitude was definitely changing.

"And what about the other questions?" Angie said, interrupting Ben's train of thought.

"Other questions?" he asked.

"Yeah. I'll get started on those first three in a minute," she laughed. "But you said you have questions for Red, too? About his guitar, I presume?"

"Oh, right. Well, the guitar, of course," he said. "But I also think there is more to the Aunt Maggie story than meets the eye. And I suspect the Strat is somehow involved."

Chapter Eleven

"*The Static*?" said Angie. "Not a bad name."

Heading east on the Pennsylvania Turnpike, Ben was anxious to re-direct the conversation. A half-hour ago Angie had innocently asked if he had any trouble taking a vacation day from work. Without thinking about it, Ben started to ramble on about the Ohio Project and his issues with upper and lower management. These things seemed very important at his desk, but as he heard himself describe the tedious office meetings, it suddenly occurred to him that listening to him talk about those meetings must be just as boring as actually participating in them. He made a mental note not to subject Angie to any more stories about Bismark Insurance.

Fortunately, she changed the topic to music by asking if he played in a band during his off hours.

He told her that he spent his teens as lead-guitarist of *The Static*, but he hadn't picked up a guitar in years. Not until Aunt Maggie's Strat arrived.

"I was twelve when I started taking lessons," he said. "I formed *The Static* with neighborhood friends a few years later. We had the usual high-school dreams of being rock stars."

"How far did you get?" she asked.

"Parties, frat houses, a couple of bars when we got older. We were pretty good. But I think we were too wrapped up with the concept of hitting it big. I remember Jamie, the other guitarist, saying that if he wasn't famous by the time he was eighteen he was going to give up. Funny, isn't it? We talked him into extending that... But by the time we were in our early 20s, the band broke up and we went our separate ways.

"Looking back on it now, the group was a lot of fun. And I don't think I appreciated that enough at the time. Of course, I wonder if you *ever* appreciate things enough at the time..."

He paused, and then continued, "Sorry for getting so philosophical. How about you?"

"I never played in a band. But I used to sneak into bars to see bands play," she said.

"Really? How young were you?"

"Sixteen...Seventeen...My parents weren't around much. They didn't notice. I loved the power of a loud rock and roll band. That's probably why I fell for Rick. It certainly wasn't his personality."

"Now we're *both* getting philosophical!" said Ben.

"Yeah, we're deep," laughed Angie.

"Anyway," she continued, "I only play guitar well enough to buy and sell them. I never took the time to actually learn."

"Maybe I can teach you a few things," he said.

"I bet you can. And maybe I can teach *you* a few things, too!" she laughed again.

Ben nervously smiled. He thought his comment was innocent enough. Perhaps hers was, too, he told himself. After all, she had already taught him a lot about Gibson Melody Makers...and the EB-1 Bass. Maybe *that's* what she meant.

Although, he thought, a girl who used to sneak into bars when she was sixteen-years-old, and who doesn't appear to have a job yet has no trouble walking around with thousands of dollars in her pocket, and at the spur of the moment accepts an offer to drive across the state in pursuit of a mystery guitar, is certainly not typical in his circle of friends. He conceded, at least to himself, that there was a lot Angie could teach him. And not just about guitars.

***

66

"Let's get back to your list," she said, "You asked about an EB-zero, right?"

"Yes, yes," he stammered, happy to return to a more comfortable conversation. "What is the real name of that bass?"

"The real name? Or what people call it?" she asked, rhetorically. "Maybe we should start with the history of that bass. After all, we *all* have a history..."

"I'm ready, professor," he said.

She smiled. "When Gibson introduced the Les Paul they wanted it to be fancier than Leo Fender's Telecaster, so they designed a guitar that was a flat piece of mahogany glued to an arched, carved maple top. Leo didn't have any carving capabilities, so this was beyond anything he could do.

"A couple of years later, they realized that they could also introduce budget guitars by just using the flat mahogany part. The flat all-mahogany guitars were the one-pickup Les Paul Junior and the two-pickup Les Paul Special."

"Was the 'Junior' smaller?" Ben asked.

"No. But good question," said Angie, "Gibson used the 'Junior' term to mean one-pickup versus two-pickup guitars."

She continued, "In the early `50s these cheaper models, the Junior and the Special, were the same silhouette as the more expensive guitar."

"Got it," he said. "Fancy guitar, or cheap guitars...same outline."

"Right," she said, "Now, here's a test. Remember when I told you that the Electric Bass was re-named the EB-1 when Gibson introduced a second bass?"

"Yes!" said Ben. "And I looked it up in the catalog. The second one was the EB-2. And it's a bass version of the 335!"

"Wow, you *have* been paying attention." Angie said, surprised. "Well, the EB-2 and the ES-335 were both introduced in 1958, and it was a really big deal. The 335 was, among other things, Gibson's first double-cutaway guitar. And it was *such* a big hit that they decided to make those cheaper guitars, the Junior and the Special, double cutaways too."

"Okay, I'm with you so far," Ben said. "In `58 the Junior and the Special changed to double cutaway."

"Good." she said. "Now, getting back to the world of basses...By the end of 1958 they decided to do away with the bass that you have, the violin-shaped EB-1, because it wasn't selling anyway. And since they now had the EB-2, a bass version of the double cutaway 335 hollow guitar, they decided to also make a bass version of the new double-cutaway solid-bodies. So they took a Les Paul Junior body and put a bass neck on it. And, ta-da, a new bass!

"It was a brand new model, and their third bass, so it should have been called an EB-3. 1, 2, 3...that would make sense. But it was just a simple slab of mahogany and pretty bare-bones, even compared to the EB-1. I guess they figured that from a fanciness standpoint they were going backwards. So they did go backwards, and named it an EB-zero."

"What a weird name," said Ben.

"I agree. But that's what it was. On paper, at least," she replied.

"But," she continued, "I wouldn't recommend saying it that way in public. I've only ever heard people call it an 'EB-Oh.' So, the long answer to a short question is: Technically it's an EB-zero, but to the world, it's an EB-Oh."

"And is that the guitar pictured in my catalog?" Ben asked, slightly confused. "The one in the catalog doesn't look bare-bones..."

"No, you're right," said Angie. "The EB-0 in the 1966 catalog is different. In 1961 Gibson decided to re-do all of their solid-bodies. They changed *everything* to the sharp-point, beveled-edge body style that we now call the 'SG.' In `61 every model...the Junior, the Special, the Les Paul Standard, the Les Paul Custom, and the EB-0...all took on the new body-shape. But that's another story. I just wanted you to know how the EB-zero, or EB-Oh, started out."

"Interesting. So the name is a toss-up, and the first version of the EB-0 bass is different than the sharp edge one in my catalog. Good stuff! Have you ever owned one of those early ones?" Ben asked.

"Only one. And I sold it years ago." said Angie. "They only made a couple hundred of them, so they're pretty rare. But those are the kind of stories that drew me into this business in the first place. The details are fascinating."

"I hope I can remember all of this," Ben said.

"Well, it's all in books. Or you can give me a call," Angie said smiling.

He smiled back. It was a lot to take in. But he loved it. And for the most part it made sense. Though he wondered how many meetings they had to have at the Gibson factory just to name that bass.

And just as he felt when he looked at the 335, 345 and 355 in the catalog, he now had a great desire to own a 1958 EB-0. And, of course, he'd have to have the 1966 version, too. This could get addictive, he told himself. But it would be so interesting to have one of everything. And unlike Angie, he'd never sell them. As he drove down the highway he wondered why there wasn't a museum somewhere, with one of every guitar model.

He supposed that different manufacturers had their own museums. And that reminded him that they were heading to the Martin factory. And Angie had a guitar to show them.

***

"By the way," he said, "Weren't you going to bring a guitar to show the Martin guys?"

69

"Yeah, it's in the back. I'm hoping they can help me figure out when it was made. It doesn't have a serial number, but it appears to be from the late 1800s... somewhere in that era."

Then, making a quick serendipitous mental connection, she added, "And now that you mention it, that ties into the EB-0 story!"

"How is that?" he asked.

"My old Martin is a Model '1-28.' Back in those days, just as they do now, Martin used the first number for the size and the second number for the level of fanciness. So in this case, the body is a Size 1, and the ornamentation is a 28."

"And how does that relate to the EB-0?" Ben asked.

"You see, dear Watson," she said, smiling, "When C.F. Martin first started making guitars, his biggest guitar was the Size 1. The next guitar in his line was the smaller Size 2. And then the even smaller Size 3."

"An odd reverse system." said Ben, "But this was before computers, so I guess any numbering system would work."

"It worked for a while," said Angie, "But eventually his customers wanted something *bigger* than a Size 1. And when folks want something bigger, you've gotta give it to them, right?"

"I'm not sure about that, but I think I see where you're going with this," he said. "Let me guess: The next biggest guitar he made was a Size zero?"

"Absolutely correct!" she said. "Just like with Gibson, he ended up going backwards. And then, when he decided to make an even bigger body?"

"If he was going backwards, mathematically it should be a Size minus-one. But I bet it's a Size 00." said Ben happily. "I know that because that's how Bob Stewart described Aunt Maggie's acoustic! He called it a 'double-Oh' but he really meant a 'double-zero'!"

"My, you *are* good!" said Angie, clearly impressed. "Do you remember everything that well? I better watch what I say around you."

"I *do* have a thing for numbers," Ben said, with just a touch of humility. "And the guitar numbers are so interesting that they're fun to remember."

"Oddly enough, I understand that," said Angie, smiling.

"And in this case," she continued, "The model name is an exact parallel to the Gibson bass. People call a Martin '00-28' a 'double-Oh 28' even though it should really be a 'double-zero-28.' I guess that's another example of how hard it is to master the English language, when we randomly interchange zeros and Os."

Ben nodded, "I do the same thing myself. My office extension is 0502, but when I give it to someone I say Oh-five-Oh-two."

They had just passed Carlisle, and would soon be switching to Route 81 toward Nazareth and Bethlehem.

"Hey," Angie said, pointing at the upcoming exit, "If you don't mind, turn off here. I want to say hello to a guy in Harrisburg."

Chapter Twelve

With Angie calling out the turns, Ben exited Route 78 and within minutes they were on West 3rd Street in Harrisburg. She asked him to pull over in front of Third Street Loan.

The building appeared to be over a hundred years old. And it looked as if the pawn shop had been there almost as long. A faded neon sign in the window blinked "Loans." Beneath the sign, hand-painted on the window glass, it read "Gold, Guns, Tools and Electronics." Behind a metal gate in the window Ben could see a selection of knives, CB radios, and electric drills, and hanging on the wall two old, dusty acoustic guitars.

As he held the door open for her, Angie said, "This won't take long." She confidently walked up to the counter as if she had been there a hundred times.

Suddenly from the back room they heard a voice, "Angie darling! I haven't seen you in years!"

The pawn shop owner, Jeffrey Jones, unhooked a small chain at the end of the counter and came around to hug Angie.

His blue t-shirt had a faded "Third Street Loan" logo and his gray hair was pulled into a small ponytail. He was roughly Ben's age.

"Hi, Jeffrey," she said, "How have you been?"

"The usual ups and downs," he said, smiling at her. "Are you going to be in town tonight? Do you want to get together?"

"No, sorry," she said. "We're just passing through. This is Ben, my driver."

Turning to shake Ben's hand, Jeffrey said, "Driver? Wow, times have changed since you used to come to town in that old Chevy Nova."

"Hey, don't knock that car. I put a lot of miles on that thing," she said.

"Those were the days," he said. Then, smiling at her again, he added, "I've missed you."

Smiling back at him, she said, "I'm not as active in the biz anymore." Reaching out to touch his arm, she added, "Besides, I'm sure you've been okay. Anything to show me today?"

As he turned back toward the counter, Jeffrey said, "Well, it's not like the old days, but come on back."

He led Ben and Angle behind the counter and into a back storage room. The room was filled with hundred-year-old wooden shelves, with the edges worn smooth from use. There were rows of rifles, radios, TVs, and just about any other item that could be pawned. Angie knew just where to turn as they walked down the aisles between the shelving.

Near the back of the building were the musical instruments. Two sets of drums, a few horns and four or five guitars. Descriptive tags with brands, model names and long pawn shop code numbers hung from the guitar case handles.

Jeffrey enthusiastically pulled a Fender case off of the shelf and opened it on a small nearby table. "You'll like this," he said. "And for you, only $900."

Angie, looked at it quickly, and said, "Thanks, but it's just a two-year-old American Standard Strat. They were only $1100 new."

Jeffrey looked at the tag on the handle, and said, "I could do $800…"

"I really appreciate it," she replied. "But it's not for me. Do you have anything older?"

"Yes, yes," he said, "Just one. I was saving this for last, but you're going to love it. A late `70s Gibson L6S."

He put the Fender case back on the shelf and pulled out a black case with a thin aluminum strip around the edge. It looked remarkably like the replacement case Ben bought for his Melody Maker all those years ago.

Jeffrey opened it and said, "These are going for big bucks now! You should be able to get $2,000 for this."

Reading his shop's code from the case handle, he said, "I can let you have it for $1,250."

Angie lifted the guitar from its case. It was a beautiful natural maple colored guitar, with three knobs and a five position rotary switch. She flipped the guitar over and looked at the back of the headstock. She turned to Jeffrey and said, "Do you mind if I look under the control panel?"

"No, of course not. Help yourself," he said.

She laid the guitar face down in its case, opened her purse and pulled out a small screwdriver, and proceeded to loosen the four Phillips-head screws on the control panel.

Jeffrey, acting as if he had seen this sort of thing before, turned to Ben and said, "How long have you known Angie?"

"A little over a week," Ben said. "She's an interesting person."

"Yeah," replied Jeffrey. "She's one-of-a-kind. I've known her for years. We've had some fun times together."

"I can hear you, you know," she said, as she lifted the control panel to look underneath.

He continued, "Angie used to buy a lot of guitars from me. But it's hard to find the good stuff anymore."

In no time Angie had the panel back in place. She turned the guitar over, straightened it out in the case, and closed the case.

Picking up her purse, she turned to the two men and said, "Jeffery, it's been lovely seeing you again. I can't use the L6S, but I'll stop back next time I'm in this neck of the woods."

"Are you sure you can't stay for dinner?" he asked.

"Sorry, we can't. We're on a quest. But thanks for showing me the guitars."

They walked back through the shelves and out into the showroom.

"Nice to meet you," said Ben as they headed to the door.

"Nice to meet you, too," said Jeffery. And then, to Angie he said, "I could probably do $1,000 on the L6S."

"I appreciate it," she said, "But not this time."

Then, as Ben opened the door, she looked back and said, "It's good to see you again, Jeffrey."

He smiled and nodded, "You, too, Angie."

***

In less than five minutes they were back on Route 78, heading north to Route 22, with Angie driving.

"Well…" said Ben, hoping that Angie would pick it up from there.

"Well, what about the guitar? Or, well, what about Jeffrey?" she asked.

"Your choice," said Ben.

"Well," she said, looking over at Ben and smiling, as if to lightheartedly mock his original 'Well.' "Back when I was buying and selling a lot of guitars I did a lot of traveling. And along the way, I'd meet people. Jeffrey's a good guy. And some really nice vintage instruments used to end up in his shop. Sometimes we'd hang out when I was passing through town."

"Hang out?" he said, with a tone that he immediately regretted. He quickly added, "Of course, it's none of my business."

"True," she said.

"With regard to the guitar," she continued, "It's fake."

"Fake?" he said, surprised.

"Yeah, I could tell almost as soon as I saw it. It's a really nice L6S copy, and whoever put the Gibson decal on it did a good job. But my immediate gut feeling was that something wasn't quite right. And then, once I looked closer..."

"What gave it away?" Ben asked.

"First of all," she said, "The plain black truss rod cover. It should have had one that said 'L6S.' Then when I turned it over, I saw that the machine heads were wrong and it had no serial number."

"No serial number is a bad sign, right?" said Ben.

"Well," said Angie, "Sometimes when you refinish a guitar you lose the serial number. And in 1976 Gibson used a serial number that was just a decal on the back of the headstock. So it could have been refinished. It didn't *look* refinished, but you never know. But checking the wiring settled it. The wiring was original to the guitar, and not Gibson's work."

"Who do you think made it?"

"I'm pretty sure it was Fujigen Gakki."

"What?" he laughed, thinking that she was making the name up.

"Fujigen Gakki. Don't you know anything about the history of guitars?" she said laughing. She knew Ben was just getting started with the history of American guitars. She didn't really expect him to know about Japanese manufacturers.

Seeing that Ben was at a loss for words, she continued, "Fujigen didn't put the Gibson decal on it. Someone else did that. But the guitar is such a high-quality copy that I'm pretty sure they were the manufacturer."

"Wow," he said.

She continued, "To give you a brief history, in the mid-1960's kids were buying guitars faster than anyone could make them. American manufacturers couldn't keep up and a lot of Japanese guitars were imported into the country. The Japanese guitars at that time were generally odd looking, cheap instruments. But they still sold a ton of them."

"Chuck, the bass player in *The Static* had a Kingston bass when we first started," said Ben. "I'm pretty sure it was made in Japan."

"It definitely was," Angie replied, nodding to him.

Continuing the story, she said, "Seeing dollar signs, big US corporations started buying up small American guitar companies. And in almost every case, quality suffered. Meanwhile in Japan, manufacturers like Fujigen Gakki continually improved the quality of their guitars. By the beginning of the 1970s they were making great copies of American guitars and by the mid-1970s some of their copies were better than the USA versions.

"Fujigen manufactured guitars for many of different Japanese brands, like Greco, Crestline, Epiphone and Ibanez. I suspect the one that we saw today was originally labeled Ibanez or Carlo Robelli. Carlo Robelli was a brand name used by the Sam Ash store in New York.

"So someone out there somewhere took a near perfect copy and changed the logo. And they probably fooled Jeffrey."

"Probably?" said Ben.

"But," she continued, "one of the first red flags with fakes is the case. For as much trouble as Fujigen and others went to copy American guitars, they never took the time to replicate the cases. A wrong case is the first warning sign."

***

Angie's knowledge of guitars continued to impress Ben. He wondered if he'd ever be able to buy a guitar without her. As he said that to himself, he realized that even if he didn't need her help with guitars, life was definitely more interesting with her around. Although he also wondered about her relationship with Jeffrey. And he wondered how many more Jeffreys there were out there.

Chapter Thirteen

Nine miles after the Route 78/Route 22 split, Angie exited Route 22 and pulled into the Holiday Inn parking lot. Tomorrow morning they were going to visit the Martin factory, and then begin their search for Red Brown.

As they were getting their bags out of the backseat, Ben for the first time saw the Martin guitar that Angie had hidden in the car's hatchback. Or at least he saw the case. And he was amazed. It was an actual wooden case. It was roughly the same shape as the guitar, but instead of the smooth curves of a modern case, it was flat pieces of wood with sharp angles. Basically a guitar-shaped wooden box, painted flat black, and covered with shipping stickers.

Seeing his surprise, Angie said, "This is how they made them back then. They used wooden boxes to ship lots of things in those days, so they probably figured that was a good way to transport your guitar. And it worked. This guy is 125 years old, and still safe in its case."

Ben threw his overnight bag over his shoulder and offered to carry the guitar. "Why, thank you sir," she said.

He carefully cradled the guitar under his arm, as they entered the hotel.

They walked to the desk, signed in and picked up their room keys. On the way to the elevator Angie turned and said, "Ben, thanks for making the stop in Harrisburg."

"No problem," said Ben, "That was fun. I've never been in the back room of a pawn shop before!"

"Well, I appreciate it," she said. "And maybe tomorrow there will be more new experiences…for both of us."

"I'm counting on it." he said, smiling.

"Meanwhile," he continued, "Shall we meet at the restaurant in a half hour for dinner?"

Angie laughed, "Let's make it an hour. And let's make it dinner and drinks."

Chapter Fourteen

Ordering the first drink was always difficult. Ben hated to mix alcohols, so his first choice would set the direction for the evening. And tonight presented yet another challenge.

Since he arrived at the Holiday Inn restaurant before Angie, Ben decided it would be a nice touch to have a drink waiting for her. He settled on a vodka martini for him and a Cosmo for her. At the very least the Cosmo would lead to interesting conversation by giving her the opportunity to accuse him of ordering the only 'girlie' drink he knew. Besides, if she didn't want it, he could always finish it himself...though he was all too aware that two martinis is generally one too many.

He kept an eye on the doorway, despite the fact that Angie would have no trouble finding him. The restaurant was nearly empty, with only one other couple and a solo traveling businessman. The kind of crowd one would expect on a weeknight in a hotel on Route 22 just outside of Bethlehem, Pennsylvania.

He was still surprised, though, when she walked through the door.

Ben's experience thus far with Angie consisted of a random meeting on a sidewalk in front of the guitar store, a drive to Ford City and back, and now a trip to Bethlehem, PA, by way of Harrisburg. These were all casual activities, and they had both dressed accordingly. So it startled him to see her walk through the door in an attractive black dress. Not particularly fancy or sexy, just a tasteful simple dress.

Seeing the look on his face as held the chair for her, she said, "Whenever I'm off on an adventure, looking for people I don't know and possibly buying an expensive guitar, I always like to pack a dress. You never know when you may need it."

"No complaints from me," he said, smiling.

The waitress arrived with two martini glasses. Looking at the drink placed in front of her, Angie smiled at Ben. "A Cosmo? A *Sex And The City* fan, I presume?" she said laughing.

"Okay," she added, as she carefully held the glass up to clink with his, "Here's to the adventure."

They spent the next hour talking about their families, friends, and life in general. Ben talked about his happy childhood, the guitar lessons at Victor Lawrence Guitar Studios that his mother would drive him to, and his adolescent dreams of being a rock star. He briefly mentioned his ten-year marriage to Jane, saying that with no kids the divorce was friendly enough.

Angie's story wasn't quite as rosy. She had an early fascination with music, but the trauma of her parent's breakup didn't allow for extravagances like music lessons. By the time Angie was in her late teens her mother had passed away and her dad had moved to California. Angie followed her love of music into a troubled relationship with a musician, and was on her own by the time she was 21.

When the topic turned back to guitars, they discussed one of the questions Ben posed at the start of the trip: Celebrity owned guitars. Angie asked if he meant 'played by a celebrity' or 'signed by a celebrity.'

"Ninety-nine percent of the celebrity-autographed guitars in the world were never played by those celebrities," she said. "In fact most of those are very cheap guitars and only signed on the pickguard, which the seller attached to a guitar later. So the famous player most likely never even touched the instrument. I remember once a guy showed me a Fender Squire Strat signed on the pickguard by Chuck Berry and he said 'Chuck used this guitar onstage in London.' Ha! Like that would ever happen."

"I've never gotten involved with autographed guitars," she continued, "That's for souvenir shops in Vegas. And the few times I've seen an autograph on an actual vintage guitar, it didn't add anything to the value. Sometimes it detracted."

"What about guitars actually used by a rock star?" Ben asked.

"Proving that is the issue," she replied. "Distinctive guitars, like Neil Young's Les Paul or Joan Jett's Melody Maker don't enter the marketplace. And if they ever *are* sold, like Eric Clapton's Strats, they're auctioned for big bucks. On the other hand, commonplace guitars, used by players who change guitars every song, are hard to authenticate. If I said, 'This is one of 300 Teles once owned by Keith Richards' I think that would be hard to prove. Unless he personally modified it or something."

Halfway through dinner they opted for another round of martinis. As the drinks were delivered, Ben said, "I may regret this."

"Hey, we're not driving anywhere tonight, so I say go for it," said Angie, "Besides, wasn't your third question about regrets?"

"No," he said, thinking back to the questions he asked at the start of the trip. "I asked if you ever wished you could go back and do it all over again..."

"You mean life so far? Would it be any different the second time?" she asked.

"I don't know. I guess that's the question. Would you change things?"

"Well, if you think about it, every decision you've ever made was based on the information you had available at that moment. We always make decisions that seem like the best idea at the time. So unless you could go back with a knowledge of the future, you'd make the same choices again, wouldn't you?"

Ben paused. "Yeah...well, I guess in this hypothetical scenario you would know what you know now..."

"So you'd know the future? Then why go back? If you know the future, why not just start now with that knowledge, and re-do tomorrow?" she said, smiling as she sipped her Cosmo.

"That's not what I meant," he said. "I mean, have you ever wished you could go back and take a different path?"

"I know what you're saying. But you wouldn't take a different path. Unless you had some inkling of the future. Unless you knew the result of one path, and therefore would retroactively choose to take the other."

"Not necessarily. What if one of your choices was random?"

"Random?" she asked. "How often are our choices random? One way or another, there is some deep motivation that sways you in one a certain direction. Don't get me wrong. I have regrets…" She looked away for a moment, thinking about her past, and the people she had known. But then, jumping back to the conversation and smiling again, she said, "I regret not buying that 1958 Les Paul Standard back in 1996. It was from early '58, so it had a goldtop finish. I knew it would never be as valuable as the later '58 sunburst Les Pauls…and it was $10,000, so I passed on it. *There's* a regret!"

He laughed. "Well, it was just a thought. I wonder if I should have pursued music, instead of locking myself behind a desk for the last 25 years."

"Look," she said, "It seemed like a good idea at the time. If you want to start changing things, start with something you *can* change, like the future."

"You're right," he said, glancing off, wondering what the future would bring.

"I like you, Ben," said Angie, catching him off guard. He looked back at her, and bumping his glass he accidentally spilled a bit of his martini.

She continued, "All of the other guys I know just want to get enough info from me to make a killing on some vintage guitar. Or they want to get to one before I do. Or," she said, again sipping at her drink, "they just want to sleep with me."

Ben smiled nervously, not knowing how to respond.

"But you," she continued, "you ask a lot of guitar questions, but not because you want to make a buck. You honestly just want to learn about them. It's like your intentions are pure of heart. And this quest to find out more about your aunt and her friends is adorable."

He could tell that the drinks were having their effect… on both of them.

"And what about that other part?" he asked.

She laughed. "Well, I guess we'll see about that."

She put her empty glass down. "It's time to call it a night. It's been a pleasure hanging with you Mr. Cooper."

"You, too, Angie."

Checking her iPhone for the time, she said, "I'll see you in the lobby at ten? The Martin factory isn't far from here."

He was a little light-headed when he got up to hold her chair. They both smiled.

"Onward to the future," said Ben. "We'll start changing it tomorrow!"

She laughed, "Maybe we already have!"

Chapter Fifteen

At 10AM in the lobby Ben had a bit of a multiple-martini headache. But Angie, standing there holding her wooden guitar case, looked fresh and ready to go.

Fifteen minutes later they were on Broad Street in Nazareth. The GPS then quickly guided them to Sycamore Street and the long, mostly one-story Martin guitar factory. In recent years Martin built a museum at the front of the building, and on the outside they replicated the façade of the original Martin factory, a few blocks away on Front Street.

As Ben and Angie entered the lobby they could see the museum entrance on their left and the check-in desk ahead. At the desk they were soon joined by David Rusk, their tour guide. Rusk was an elderly, white-haired gentleman, formerly a sales rep, and now leading tours.

Ben was amazed by the tour. Walking across the factory floor, they passed by craftsmen sanding and assembling assorted pieces of wood. Others were carefully fitting necks to bodies. They stood a few feet from a woman delicately installing tiny pieces of pearl around the sound hole of a D-45. He laughed to himself, as he imagined tours being led through his office while he was at his desk.

Later in the tour they were shown Martin's CNC machines, where bodies and necks were cut from raw lumber. Other computerized machines handled buffing. The entire factory was an interesting combination of new and old technology.

As they were completing their tour Angie mentioned her old Martin to David. He said that he'd love to see it. She retrieved it from the car and they took it to a small conference room near the museum.

"Beautiful 'coffin case,'" he said as she placed the wooden case on the table. "You know, C.F. Martin made these cases as well as the guitars."

Ben had yet to see the actual guitar, so he edged in closer as David opened the case. David pointed out the small paper label attached to the inside top of the case. "Here's the model information."

The label read:

C.F. MARTIN & CO.

MANUFACTURERS OF GUITARS, etc.

Size of G. No. of Qual.

Under the "Size of G." was a handwritten 1 and under the "No. of Qual." was written 28.

"It's a model 1-28," said David. "The 1 is its size designation, and the 28 is its 'Quality' level, as the tag reads. But in those days that was also the price. This guitar cost $28 when it was new."

"And when exactly was that?" Angie asked. "I know it's from the late 1800s, but that was before you used serial numbers."

"That's easy enough," David said, as he turned to a nearby drawer and pulled out a small battery-powered light-up mirror on an extendable handle.

He switched on the lighted mirror and gently slid it between the strings. Once the mirror was in the soundhole, he tilted it so that the light shown on the underside of the top of the guitar. Moving toward the treble side, he searched for a second and said, "There it is. 1874. It's even initialed by the shop foreman."

David stepped back, still holding the mirror in place. Angie and Ben leaned in.

"It's backwards, of course, since we're looking in a mirror. But you can see the handwritten '1874' and 'S.D.' for Samuel Dietrich," said David.

Angie and Ben both leaned in closer to view the reflection in the small mirror, and their heads brushed together. Seeing markings written inside the guitar, pencil scratches from almost 150 years ago, amazed them both. Simultaneously they leaned slightly back, and looked at each other…still so close that their noses almost bumped.

With their faces nearly touching they both froze. Then Angie broke the ice, saying to Ben, "The 1870s! And I thought the 1970s were a long time ago."

Ben laughed off the situation, but deep inside he enjoyed the closeness of the moment.

As they both straightened up David said, "If you ever want to sell it, let us know. It's in beautiful shape." As he strummed the guitar he added, "Sounds great, too."

Angie said, "This case probably helped it survive."

"That's true," said David, "It's interesting to imagine it being shipped from the factory to the customer in that."

"It probably bounced around a few wagons on the way," said Ben.

"I'm sure it did. Though on longer trips it probably went by train. I can picture this packed in a freight car with other wooden boxes," said David, with a nostalgic tone to his voice.

Picking up on it immediately, Ben said, "Are you a train fan?"

"Well…old-time ones."

"And do you have a train set at home?"

Surprised at the guess, David said, "Yes, how did you know?"

"I'm not sure," said Ben, "but here's another question for you. Do you know a guy named Red Brown? He's an old family friend."

"Red, from over in Bethlehem? Sure."

Ben looked over at Angie. She smiled.

David continued, "I haven't seen him for a few months. But I know where he lives."

Chapter Sixteen

Time. Ben couldn't get it out of his head.

They were in the parking lot of the current Martin factory in Nazareth, Pennsylvania. Less than a mile from that spot, in the original Martin factory, over a century ago shop foreman Samuel Dietrich picked up a pencil and on the underside of a guitar's top, wrote his initials and the date. Now, in a future that Dietrich could never have imagined, a future that includes electricity, automobiles, radio, television, computers and the internet, that guitar is still being played. And it plays and sounds as perfect as the day it was made.

Ben's mother had bought him his first guitar, the Gibson Melody Maker in 1972. Over forty years ago. So long ago that it now seems like a distant dream. In moments they would be heading to Red Brown's house, a man that Ben's Aunt Maggie met in 1957. Over sixty years ago. Before Ben was born. And along the way they are traveling with a guitar made in 1874. Over one hundred and forty years ago.

Time was speeding by him. Yet there was no way to see it. In minutes he'd be steering the car down Route 191. He'd see the passing guardrails, and the telephone poles, and the houses. All of the indications that they are moving forward in distance. But where are the indicators of time? Where are time's signposts?

Changes in time were all around him. The memories of his past. The guitars and notes left behind by Aunt Maggie. He could *feel* that things were different. Last night's dinner with Angie had stirred emotions that he hadn't felt in years. But now, a day later, even that felt like a dream.

What if we could see time the way we see distance, he wondered.

"Hey! Are you gonna start this car or what?" Angie said, shaking Ben from his mental wanderings.

Quickly bringing himself back to reality Ben said, "Oh, ah, yeah, sorry. I'm ready. Which way are we heading?"

"Turn left at the end of the parking lot," she said.

Then she added, "You almost kissed me back there, when we bumped heads looking into that soundhole, didn't you?"

Ben, completely surprised by her comment, considered denying it. That would have been his natural response. But after his mental trip through time and space, he felt that there was no point in wasting the 'time' that he was traveling through.

"Yes."

"I thought so," she replied. "Well, maybe the next time we're looking at a lighted mirror inside an old guitar."

Ben didn't know what to think of Angie. She constantly surprised him. She had an encyclopedic knowledge of vintage guitars, and a self-confidence he had never encountered before, in a man or woman.

"Tell me something I don't know about guitars," he asked. He loved listening to her talk about guitars. Yes, it was an odd thing to base a relationship on. But it was *their* thing, and he loved it.

"What's the topic?" she asked.

"I don't know," he said. "First ever electric guitar…"

"Hawaiian or Spanish?" she asked.

"What do you mean?" he said. "Like an African versus European Swallow?" he added, referencing a scene from *Monty Python And The Holy Grail*.

"Ha! I loved that movie!" she said, "'It's just a flesh wound!'"

He smiled as she referenced yet another scene from the movie. He was happy to have her on this trip. He was happy to have her in his life.

And all thanks to late Aunt Maggie, someone he hadn't spoken to in three decades. 'Time' again. It was everywhere.

"For some reason," Angie said, switching back to his question, "back in the old days they described guitars that are played the way we normally play a guitar, vertically against your chest, as 'Spanish Guitars'. Compared to a Hawaiian guitar that you would play in your lap, horizontally. I don't know what's up with the 'Spanish' part. I guess I should learn more about that."

"Okay…" he hesitantly said, waiting for more info.

"Anyway," she continued, "The first commercially produced electric guitar was a Hawaiian guitar, the Rickenbacker 'Frying Pan' in 1931. The first electric 'Spanish guitar' was Lloyd Loar's ViviTone in 1933. And the first electric 'Spanish' *solidbody* was Rickenbacker again in 1934."

"Not Gibson or Fender?"

"What?" she said, pretending to be disappointed. "Come on, Ben, don't embarrass me in front of the old Martin in the back seat."

"Sorry…" he laughed.

She continued, "Gibson was a big corporation, even back in 1931. They weren't going to jump on some new-fangled fad, like electricity. And Leo hadn't opened his first radio shop yet. He was still working as an accountant."

"What's up with the questions anyway?" she added.

"I don't know. I just like listening to you talk."

"Well then listen to this: Turn left onto Spruce Street. It's the third house on the right."

***

Back at the Martin factory, David Rusk had given them directions to Red Brown's house. David knew Red through a model train collectors group. Ben was a little surprised that David would share that information with two strangers, but apparently Ben and Angie looked innocent enough that David accepted their 'Red is a family friend' explanation.

As they got out of the car Angie asked, "Is Red even going to know who you are?"

"Good question. Only if Aunt Maggie mentioned me. But I don't know why she would."

Their knock on the door was answered by a tall, handsome man in his late 20s.

"Yes?" he asked.

"Hi," said Ben, "Is this the Brown residence?"

An elderly voice came from the kitchen, "Who's at the door?"

Yelling toward the kitchen, he said, "I've got it Grandma." He then turned back to Ben and Angie and said, "What can I do for you?"

Ben could see the skepticism in his eyes. He was clearly protective of his grandmother.

In an effort to explain the situation Ben reached into his pocket and unfolded the note that had been hidden in the Strat. Holding it out, he said, "My name is Ben Cooper, from Pittsburgh. And this note is from my Aunt Maggie. She was a friend of Red's. She sent me to help him with a guitar."

Looking down at the note, puzzled by its cryptic message, he said, "Hi. I'm Steve. Steve Richards."

Slowly walking up behind him appeared an 84-year-old woman. "What is it, Steve?" she asked.

"It's a message about Grandpa," he said, handing her the note. "From someone named Maggie…"

"Oh my," she said, stopping in her tracks.

Looking up at Ben and Angie, she said, "Come in. Come in."

Steve stepped aside and the four of them sat down in the living room.

"I'm Ruth, Red's wife. It was so nice of Maggie to send you here. How is she?"

A little embarrassed by the question, Ben said, "Oh… I'm sorry. Maggie passed away last month. But she left this note for me. She wanted me to help Red."

"Oh dear," said Ruth. Ben could see the sadness in her eyes.

In a comforting tone, Ben said, "Were you and Maggie close?"

With a tear in her eye, Ruth nodded.

She dabbed her eye with a tissue, looked down and said, "We knew she wasn't well. She wanted to come up and visit, to see Elizabeth one last time."

Ben and Angie looked at each other, sharing the same confused thought. Who is Elizabeth?

Steve moved next to his grandmother and put his arm around her. She continued, "And then Red passed…"

Ben and Angie again silently looked at each other.

"That was six weeks ago. I called her to tell her. I wondered why she didn't come for the funeral. Now I know."

"I'm so sorry Mrs. Brown," Angie said softly, speaking for the first time.

Her eyes red, Ruth looked at Angie, and said, "Thank you, dear."

She looked back at Ben. Still sad, but this time with a touch of frustration in her voice, she added, "And then there's the issue with that guitar…"

Chapter Seventeen

Mrs. Brown led Ben and Angie into her kitchen.

"Come, I'll make you some lunch."

Turning to her grandson Steve, she said, "Run down to the shop and get your mother. Tell her we have visitors."

"I'm so sorry to hear about your husband, Mrs. Brown," said Ben as he took his seat at the kitchen table.

"Thank you dear," she said, as she gathered some plates and utensils. "And please, call me Ruth."

At first Ben and Angie were at a loss for words. Their search to find Red had been quite an adventure. They were surprised to learn that he had passed away. Finally Ben said, "We had a very pleasant visit with Bob Stewart last week, Ruth. He spoke very highly of Red."

"Bob was in Maggie's band, wasn't he?" she said. "I only met him once or twice. But, yes, Red was a wonderful man. Red and I met in first grade. He was my first boyfriend."

"Wow," said Angie.

"Well, we didn't start dating right away." Ruth laughed. "But we did get pretty serious right after high school. Then…" She glanced up from the sandwiches she was making, looking off into the distance.

Catching herself, she looked back down, resumed her work on the sandwiches, and said, "Well, you know how couples are. We went our separate ways for a few years. Then, when the thing with Maggie happened, we got back together. I haven't regretted a day since."

"Oh…" she continued, "except for the day with the guitar."

Looking up at them she said, "Elizabeth will be here soon to scold me about it again. But I know she'll be glad to see you."

Ben was now seriously confused.

"I apologize," he said, "But I'm afraid I don't know what's going on. Should I know Elizabeth?"

A bit surprised, Ruth looked at him and said, "I'm so sorry. I thought that was one of the reasons you came here. But I guess Maggie didn't tell you."

"Maggie's note only mentioned the guitar," Ben said. "I presumed she wanted me to help Red sell it."

"Well, that would have been nice..." Ruth said hesitantly. "Elizabeth's antique shop is just barely getting by, and Steve is in med school, and now with Red gone... We could have used the money..."

Just then Ben heard the front door open and close. In walked a casually dressed, attractive middle-aged woman. With a smile on her face she hugged Ruth and said, "Hi, Mom."

Turning to Ben and Angie, she said, still speaking to Ruth, "Steve said you had company. They're not in the guitar business, I hope."

Standing up and reaching out to shake her hand, Ben said, "I'm Ben Cooper, and this is Angie. My late Aunt Maggie sent us here to help Red with a guitar."

Elizabeth turned back to Ruth and said, "Late?"

Holding Elizabeth's hand, Ruth said, "I'm sorry dear. I know she wanted to see you. But she wasn't well."

Looking down with a sad look on her face, Elizabeth was silent for a moment. Then she hugged Ruth again, and said, "Well, *we* have each other." Looking over to take Ben's hand, she added, "And now I have my cousin."

Letting go of Elizabeth's hand, Ben sat back down, trying to process the information. 'Cousin?' he thought.

95

Seeing the puzzled look on his face, Ruth said, "Maggie didn't just send you here to help me and Red. She sent you to help her daughter."

Suddenly putting it all together, Ben looked up at Elizabeth and said, "Were you born in 1960?"

"It's not really polite to ask a woman's age," she said, with a bit of a smile.

"Yes," said Ruth. "Maggie and Red were very close friends. They had their fling, but they weren't in love."

Still facing Ruth, Ben's eyes darted over to meet Angie's eyes, and then back to Ruth.

"It was a different time... and in those days Maggie could not have made it as a single mom. So, when she discovered her condition, we all moved here from Michigan. To get a fresh start. Red and I got married, and when Elizabeth was born we raised her as our own. And Maggie went back to her life on the road with her band."

"Maggie came to visit whenever she could," said Elizabeth. "I knew her as Aunt Maggie. Mom...Ruth...told me the truth when I was a teenager."

"And Maggie never told anyone?" asked Ben, "Not the guys in the band or her family? Not even my dad, her brother?"

"No," said Ruth. "It was very hard for her, but she loved Elizabeth as much as Red and I did. She wanted Elizabeth to have a wonderful, normal childhood."

"And I did!" said Elizabeth.

"Well, this certainly is not what I expected," said Ben.

They sat in silence for a moment, as Ben glanced away, processing this new information. He flashed back to the last time he saw Aunt Maggie, decades ago, at the family reunion. Back then he thought she was just another older relative. When you're eighteen the world revolves around you. You never think that other folks have issues, problems, secrets. But Maggie had a secret. A big one. He hoped that he didn't say anything stupid or insensitive back then, but as an adolescent it's hard to avoid that. He wished he could go back in time and have an actual conversation with Maggie.

But he remembered what Angie said last night. You can't change the past, only the future.

He turned back to Elizabeth. "It's nice to meet you Cousin Elizabeth."

"You, too, Cousin Ben."

After a quick smile he said, "Now, what's the story with the guitar?"

"It's not a good one," said Elizabeth.

Chapter Eighteen

"We hadn't looked at that guitar for thirty years," said Ruth. "Then a couple of months ago Maggie and Red were talking on the phone and she mentioned it. I think he forgot he even had the old thing. So, he got it out, looked at it for a day or two and left it in the guest room. And that's where it stayed.

"Then, a few days after Red's funeral, a man knocked on my door. He said he had a store in Philadelphia, and he was looking for old guitars. So I let him look at it.

"He told me that it might be valuable, but he would have to have it appraised. He seemed like such nice man, that I let him take the guitar."

Looking over at Elizabeth, she added, "I know, I know. It was a mistake. But he seemed so nice, and he gave me a receipt."

Elizabeth had a frustrated look on her face, but Ben could tell that she had already discussed it repeatedly with her mother.

Angie finally spoke up, "Can we see the receipt?"

"Sure," said Elizabeth, "But we called the phone number and it's disconnected. We tried writing to him, but that letter came back with 'No Such Address' on it. I'm afraid the guitar is gone."

Ruth reached into a kitchen drawer, and pulled out a folded piece of paper.

Angie unfolded it and looked at the name: Mick's Vintage Guitars. The address was a post office box in Philadelphia. In the middle of the receipt it said, "Taking Gibson guitar for appraisal." It was signed by "Mick Bilco." She had never heard of the store or the dealer. She looked at the back of the paper. Not part of a typical two-part store receipt, it looked more like a homemade receipt printed on everyday 20-pound paper.

She looked back up at Ruth. "Can you tell me anything about him?"

"Well," said Ruth, "He was kind of heavy, and he had gray hair and was a little balding."

"That narrows him down to almost *every* vintage dealer," Angie said quietly to Ben.

Ben could see that Elizabeth and Ruth had given up on the guitar. But he could also see the look in Angie's eyes. He guessed that this man was an unscrupulous dealer who checked obituaries when he passed through a town, with the hope of doing exactly what he did with Ruth. And Ben could see Angie's anger growing. She had spent a significant part of her life buying and selling guitars. And in the guitar business, like any business, there are good guys and bad guys. Ben could tell that Angie did not want this bad guy to get away.

Ben turned back to Ruth. "Do you remember any of your conversation with him?"

"Hmmm…" she said, thinking back to the day. "He said that he wondered if the guitar was real. I don't know what he meant by that. Red never played it, but it was definitely a real guitar."

"Anything else?" asked Ben.

"Oh," she said, suddenly remembering, "He said he owned a lot of guitars, even one that used to belong to Elvis!"

"That might help," Ben said. He turned to Angie, "Any ideas?"

"Well, we need to know what guitar we're looking for. The receipt only says 'Gibson.' Do you know what model it was?" she asked Ruth.

Ruth looked confused. "No. No I don't. It was electric, I know that."

Ben asked, "Do you remember when Red got it?"

"I'm not sure," said Ruth. "One of his friends at the factory gave it to him as a thank you gift. In 1961, maybe?"

"A thank you gift?" asked Angie.

"Yes," said Ruth, as her memories of the past started getting clearer. "It was a thank you gift because Red drew it.

"Red was a designer, and a few years earlier...maybe 1957 or 58...they asked him for some new ideas for different guitar shapes and he did some sketches. I don't know what ever happened with them, but a few years later they gave him this guitar. Red just put it away."

Ben could suddenly feel pain in his forearm. He looked down to see Angie squeezing it as she followed Ruth's every word.

"What was it shaped like?" Angie asked, with an odd restrained tone to her voice.

"I don't know... kind of square, with some points, I suppose," said Ruth.

Still squeezing Ben's forearm, Angie calmly said, "Would you excuse us for a moment?"

They got up and she slowly led him back into the living room.

Once they were around the corner, her grip tightened even further. She looked him right in the eye, and whispered, "We've got to find this guitar! This is important."

"What do you think it is?" Ben whispered back.

Before she could answer, they heard a voice from the dining room. Ruth had gone out the other kitchen door, into the dining room. "I have the case, if that helps."

As she entered the living room, she said, "I didn't know where the case was when the man was here. Red had left the guitar out, but put the case away. I only found it last week, under his train set in the attic."

Angie let go of Ben and walked over to the brown rectangular case. "May I look inside?"

Ben was amazed at how calm she seemed on the outside. He knew her blood was racing on the inside.

100

Angie placed the case flat on the couch. She opened it and stared at the empty pink felt lining. There, impressed in the lining, was the outline of a guitar. A guitar so rare that most experts don't believe it even exists.

Angie was speechless. She turned toward Ben to explain, but no words came out. Before he could ask her what she was thinking, Ruth spoke up again.

"I also found the book that came with it…"

Angie turned, as Ruth handed her a faded ledger book. Angie opened it to a bookmarked page, and scanned down to a circled guitar and serial number. She closed the book and sat down on the couch in disbelief. It was the missing late-1958 Gibson factory "Day Book." A book as important as the guitar. Maybe more important. The book that would prove everything.

Chapter Nineteen

Ben was impressed with Angie's self-control.

As she paged through the 1958 Gibson log book in the Brown family living room, Ben could see her hands trembling slightly. She calmly looked up at Mrs. Brown, and with a hesitation in her voice that only he noticed, she said, "Did your husband receive this book with the guitar?"

Ruth said, "Yes. It was in the case."

Angie took a moment to close the book and slowly put it in the empty guitar case. She stood up and reached out to shake Ruth's hand with both of hers. She said, "I'm sorry that I never had a chance to know Red. Or Maggie. But it has been so nice to meet you and your family. Ben and I will find this guitar. I promise."

Though he had no idea what guitar they would be looking for, nor did he understand the significance of the book, Ben sensed Angie's determination. If she thought they could find the guitar, he wouldn't doubt her.

He picked up Maggie's note that Ruth had left next to the TV. The note that had been hidden in Maggie's Stratocaster. Now his Stratocaster. As he folded the piece of paper and put it back in his pocket he said, "Maggie asked us to help, and we will."

He hugged Ruth and his new-found cousin, Elizabeth, and he and Angie walked silently to the car. Angie carried the empty guitar case.

With the case safely stored in the back seat of the car, Angie got in the passenger side. As soon as Ben got behind the wheel and closed the door, Angie reached over and good-naturedly punched him in the arm.

"Ha!" she said. "You wanted to learn about vintage guitars? How about learning something that *no one else in the world* knows!"

Ben laughed. "I think with this one you'd better start at the beginning."

Looking forward, into the distance, she shook her head side to side and smiled. "Ben Cooper, I can't believe what you've gotten us into."

He could tell that she was stunned. Too stunned to immediately begin the explanation that would make everything clear to him. But he didn't want to start the car yet. This story was going to need his undivided attention.

Angie's mind was still racing, but she looked at him, smiled and said, "Okay... from the beginning..."

He smiled back. He loved her vintage guitar stories. And this one was clearly going to be a doozy.

"It starts with Leo Fender, in 1950," she said. "Leo shook up the music world with his new solid-body electric guitar. There were some name issues in the beginning, but he soon called it the 'Telecaster.'

"When sales started taking off for the Telecaster, Gibson saw that there was money to be made with the solid-body concept. So they decided they'd better jump on that bandwagon, too. In 1952 they introduced *their* solid-body, the 'Les Paul.'

"And all was right in the world. The Les Paul versus the Telecaster."

"I know those two models," said Ben. "Everyone has heard of them."

"Right," said Angie. "But in the early 50s the little guy, Leo, and big corporation, Gibson, had different thoughts about what should come next."

"Over the next two years, Gibson introduced different versions of the Les Paul: The budget versions, the Les Paul Special and Les Paul Junior, and a fancier version, the Les Paul Custom.

"But Leo Fender designed a totally new guitar, the Stratocaster, which was fun, different and exciting.

"To the public it looked like Leo was the hip, young innovator. And Gibson was a boring, stodgy corporation.

"So in 1957, some folks at Gibson decided to show the world that they could shake things up, too. They started sketching up some weird, oddball shaped guitars. Odder than anything else on the market. And they patented three of them. The patents just show the shape of the guitars, they don't have any model names, but Gibson described these new designs as their 'Modernistic' guitars. Ha! They were self-describing themselves as a 'Modern' company."

"Were they the self-described 'King-of-Pop...ular Guitars'?" Ben interrupted.

Angie laughed out loud, and then replied, "And are you self-describing yourself as 'funny'?"

He laughed back.

She continued, "Anyway, there were plans for three Modernistic models." She held up three fingers. "They would be made from a light-colored wood that Gibson called 'Korina.' In early 1958 they started shipping the *first* design, shaped like a sideward V, so they called it the 'Flying V.'

"And here's where it gets interesting. Gibson's log-book for the first half of 1958 lists the manufacture of 52 Flying Vs. And they planned to make the *other* Modernistic guitars in the second half of 1958, but..."

"But?" asked Ben.

"But the book for the second half of 1958 is missing! The only thing Gibson has in their possession is a list of their *total* production of different models made in 1958. That yearly-total sheet lists all of the Flying Vs for the year...a total of 81, by the way."

Angie started smiling again.

She continued, "Plus that sheet lists 19 other Modernistic guitars that were made during the second half of the year. But they aren't itemized. They are all combined under the general title: 'Korina(Mod. Gtr).'"

"I think I'm following," Ben said. "During the year they made 81 Flying Vs and 19 other Modern guitars…But the yearly sheet doesn't specify which models the other 19 were."

"Right," said Angie. "Now we know, based on what have turned up over the years, that most of those 19 were the *second* Modernistic guitar, the one eventually called the 'Explorer.' But were they ALL Explorers? Or did they also make the *third* model?"

"I don't know. Did they?" Ben asked.

"Well," she replied, "We've never known. No one has ever seen a guitar from 1958 that matches the third patent. Despite that, by the 1970s this potential third guitar, the mystery one, became known as the 'Moderne.'"

"That's a weird name," said Ben.

"I agree," said Angie. "BUT…" she said, raising her voice, "everything changes today!"

At that point Angie turned around, hopping up with her knees on the seat, as she reached into the back seat. She flipped up the latches on the case and pulled out the book Ruth had handed her.

Spinning around, she put the book in her lap and started paging through it.

"And that is?" asked Ben.

"The missing log book from the second half of 1958!" she said excitedly, still paging. "Red Brown has had it in his attic since 1960!"

She stopped on the page for a day in late July.

The lined paper had handwritten lists of dates, model names, and serial numbers.

"Look, right here," she said pointing.

The entry read: *Modern 2*   And the 2 had a line drawn through it, and the word *Explorer* was written next to it.

"This guitar was originally entered as 'Modern 2,' before it was corrected to 'Explorer,'" she said.

Then she flipped ahead to a page in September that had been bookmarked.

"Look! Look!" she said.

This entry was easy to find since it had long ago been circled.

Ben looked closely and saw that the guitar was entered as: 'Modern 3'.

He looked back up at Angie, as she stared right into his eyes.

"They DID make a Moderne," she said, "But it isn't 'Moderne' after all. It's just 'Modern 3'! Modern guitar #3!! And Red Brown, your Red Brown, was a designer. He must have designed that model for Gibson. And they made one! And it never sold, so they gave it to him!"

"But why wouldn't it have sold?" Ben asked.

"All of these Modernistic guitars were a failure," she said. "They were too far ahead of their time. Gibson stopped making them almost immediately. They didn't reissue the V until the late 1960s and the Explorer until the mid-1970s."

"So the guitar that Ruth gave away is a one-of-a-kind guitar?"

"Yes, and not only one-of-a-kind, but one-of-a-kind that no one knows exists." she said. "We've *got* to get this guitar back."

"And how are we going to do that?" he asked.

"I'm not sure," she said. "But I know a lot of vintage dealers. And most of them are great guys. This guy is a lying thief. He'll stand out. We'll find him."

"But, where?"

"Wait a minute," she suddenly said. "What day is this?"

Without waiting for an answer, she pulled out her phone and looked up a web site. She scanned down the page and turned to Ben.

"Start the car. We're heading to Valley Forge."

Chapter Twenty

Ben checked his watch. Then he glanced over at Angie in the passenger seat.

She was intently reading, page by page, the July '58 through December '58 Gibson log book, and making notes on the back of a tour catalog from the Martin Guitar Museum they had visited earlier in the day.

Based on the time, 3 pm, and the fact that they were heading south from Bethlehem, PA to Valley Forge, PA, it was clear that they would not make it back to Pittsburgh this evening. And he would not be there for tomorrow morning's project manager meeting.

He'd have to call the office and let them know. The Ohio Project would have to continue without him.

Normally missing a meeting at work would have made Ben nervous. But today he couldn't get something out of his mind. It was a question he saw on Reddit.com the night before he and Angie left on this trip. He liked to check the site every day or two for news, TILs (Things I Learned), AMAs (Ask Me Anything), and general updates on current topics and trends. After all, it is called the "Front Page Of The Internet."

On the site folks occasionally post random questions to the Reddit community under the AskReddit heading. Two days ago someone asked, "What Is The Worst Thing You've Done For Money?" Predictably, many of the responses described things that were questionable on moral, ethical or legal levels. But one reply stuck with Ben: What is the worst thing I've done for money? I traded away forty hours of my life every week for forty years. Those years are gone.

The comment hit Ben too close to home. Had he traded away too much of his life? Both sides of the argument were obvious. He needed money to survive, and he needed a job to get the money. On the other hand, the most valuable thing in life, the thing that money can't buy, is time. Where is the balance? 'I give you my life, or at least a portion of it, and you give me cash.' That was the deal he'd struck with Bismark. But was it a good deal?

He knew that worrying about the past served no useful purpose, but here, on Route 476 in eastern Pennsylvania, he decided that his job at Bismark Insurance would *not* dictate his future. Aunt Maggie's request had put him on this path, and he was going to follow through, no matter what.

Besides, thanks to Aunt Maggie, he now had a beautiful 1956 Strat; a rare 1954 Gibson Electric Bass; new-found friends in Bob and Mary Stewart; a newly-discovered Cousin Elizabeth; and a chance to help both Elizabeth and Red Brown's wife Ruth by tracking down a missing guitar. Plus he met someone who has not only rekindled his interest in guitars, but his excitement about life in general… Angie.

Glancing over at her, he wasn't sure how Angie felt about him. But he had never seen someone so fascinated by a ledger book that consisted of nothing more than line after line of handwritten dates, model names, and serial numbers. Eventually, she closed the book and looked up at him.

"I checked every page," she said. "I found four other instances where the model name was originally entered as 'Modern 2' and then changed to 'Explorer.' And then for the rest of the book those models are only listed as 'Explorer.' There are 18 entries like that. And only one listed as 'Modern 3.'

"And everything adds up to just what you'd expect. Those 18 entries for 'Explorer,' plus our guitar make the total 19."

"That was the mystery number, right?" Ben asked.

"Right," she said. "We knew that this book, the missing book, contained 29 Flying Vs and 19 other 'Modernistic' guitars. Now we know the exact breakdown of those 19.

"When you think about it, they must have been pretty disappointed at the factory," she continued. "With the Flying Vs, for example, they sold 52 during the first six months, and then only 29 during the next six months. The other two models were complete failures."

"Was that it for those guitars?" asked Ben.

"No," said Angie. "They sold a few more the following year. In 1959 they sold 17 more Vs and 3 more Explorers. They still have the books for that year, so we already knew those numbers."

"So the totals are?"

"Do you mean what the rest of the world thinks? Or what *we* now know to be the *truth*??" she asked with a wide grin.

She continued, "Until today the numbers were 98 Vs and 22 Explorers. But we know the *real* numbers are 98, 21 and 1."

Ben laughed.

"By the way," he asked, "Where are we going?"

"Oh, I'm so sorry. I got carried away with the log book," she said. "We're heading to the Philadelphia Expo Mart, near Valley Forge. There's a guitar show this weekend. We can look for our guy."

"A guitar show?" he asked, although he knew the Monroeville Convention Center near his house hosted coin shows, pet shows and comic book conventions. It stood to reason that there would be guitar shows.

Angie answered, "The first ever guitar show was a very small affair in Texas in 1978. Just a handful of guys getting together to look at guitars. By the mid-1980s, though, the concept grew and spread across the country. Dealers and buyers would come from all over the world to buy, sell, and trade guitars. During the guitar show heyday, in the mid-1990s, you could go to a show every weekend somewhere in the US. They've slowed down a lot in recent years, but the Philly Show, the one we're going to, is still great. If nothing else, you'll be able to look at a couple thousand guitars."

"Really?"

"Really. Now, if you don't mind, pull over to that Walmart just ahead."

Ben stayed in the car while Angie quickly ran into the store. A few minutes later she returned with a box of large trash bags and an inexpensive shoulder purse just big enough to carry the Gibson log book.

Climbing back into the car, she said, "The purse is for the book, so it can stay with us. I'll explain the trash bags later."

Angie clearly knew what she was doing, so Ben just nodded and headed back on the highway.

By 5 pm they were parking the car outside the Expo Center entrance. The outside was dark, and there were only a few people around.

"Are we too late?" he asked.

"No, this is dealer set-up day. You need badge to get in. The show won't be open to the public until tomorrow."

She opened the hatchback of the Subaru and grabbed her old Martin in its odd wooden case. Handing the Martin to Ben, she moved Red Brown's empty case from the backseat to the rear of the car, where it would be hidden from view in the hatchback. The long brown case barely fit. She put the Gibson log book in the newly purchased purse, threw it over her shoulder, and with Ben carrying the Martin they headed toward the Expo entrance.

As they approached the hall Ben could see a check-in desk and beyond it a huge open room. Just as Angie predicted, there were hundreds of tables, filled with guitars. Dealers were busy setting up guitar stands and adding more guitars to their tables.

"I hope Dusty is here today," he heard her mutter to herself.

When they reached the check-in desk the lady collecting dealer payments and issuing badges looked up, smiled, and said, "Angie! Good to see you again! It's been years. Do you have a booth?"

"It's nice to see you, too, Sandy," Angie said casually. "We're here to help Dusty. He has our badges."

"Oh, no problem," said Sandy, "Go on in." She waved to the guard at the door, indicating that their badges were inside.

Ben quickly understood the situation. He smiled at Sandy, and carrying the Martin, followed Angie.

Once safely in the room, Angie turned to Ben and said, "Dealers get two badges with one booth, three with two booths, and so on. Dusty always buys three booths, but travels by himself, so he usually has extra badges. I was guessing that he'd be here."

Three or four steps later, Ben heard a loud, laughing Southern accent, "Angie, darlin'! Are you back in the business?"

Angie rushed over to the tall man with a smiling, happy face and a bushy moustache. She gave him a big hug, and whispered in his ear, "Any extra badges for us, dear?"

"For you, anything," he replied.

As they separated from the hug, Dusty held both of her hands, and said, "You look fabulous!" Looking up at Ben, who was just now getting to the booth, Dusty added, "Is this your fella? Am I gonna hav'ta fight him for your love?"

"Come off it, Dusty," she said, "I know you're married now."

"I can still dream, can't I?" he said.

"This is Ben," she said.

Dusty reached out to shake Ben's hand, "Howdy. What's in the case?"

112

Before Ben could answer, Angie said, "That's an old 1-28. Do you mind if I stash it under your table? I don't want to leave it in the car."

"You can leave anything under my table..." he said, with a wink.

Angie shook her head and smiled. "You'll never change, Dusty."

"Don't wanna," he laughed.

He reached into his shirt pocket and handed them each a dealer badge.

Angie then stepped in closer, and touched Dusty's arm. She looked around at the other dealers who were busy setting up their booths for tomorrow's opening and lowered her voice. "I need to talk to you about something."

Dusty's multiple-booth setup was arranged in an elongated u-shape. He led her and Ben over to a corner, out of ear-shot of other dealers. He could see that she was serious. "What can I do for you?"

"Ben and I are looking for a guitar that was stolen from an old lady. A guy gave her a fake receipt, and probably a fake name, but I don't think he was an amateur. I think someone here will know him."

Despite Dusty's previous lighthearted comments, Ben could see that he respected Angie, and wanted to help.

"Oww," he said, "That's bad. What kind of guitar is it?"

Just then they heard Sandy's voice loudly over the intercom, "We are closing for the day. Please exit the building. The show opens tomorrow at 9 am for dealers and 10 am for the public. See you tomorrow."

Dusty said, "Where are you staying? I'll be at the Marriott right down the road. Most of the dealers are there. Why don't you meet me at the hotel bar in a half hour. We'll talk about it there."

Angie slid her old Martin under his table, leaned up and gave Dusty a kiss on the cheek. "Thanks, babe. We'll see you at the bar."

***

Ben and Angie walked back to the car and made the short trip down the road. The hotel was buzzing as all of the dealers from the show arrived almost simultaneously. Ben joined the line at check-in as Angie stayed in the parking lot, sliding a large trash bag over each end of the empty Modern 3 guitar case. She tied the bags in the middle, at the case handle.

When Ben finally got to the receptionist, he learned that there was only one room left in the hotel. Fortunately, it had two beds. Old Ben would have worried. New Ben, the new take-life-as-it-comes Ben, took the room. He knew Angie's philosophy would be "We'll figure it out." He was trying his best to adopt her attitude.

He met her as she was entering the lobby. "Room 305," he said.

"Great," she said. Carrying the guitar case, she headed straight for the elevator.

Once they were on the elevator, he finally asked, "What's with the trash bags?"

She said, "This is a late 1950s rectangular Gibson case. It's a legitimate case from the Lifton factory, but you can still see that it's a prototype. There are not many guitars that would fit in this case, and I didn't want one of these dealers to recognize it from across the room. That would require too much explaining on our part. I know it looks funny with the bags over it, but with this crowd, it's better to look funny than super-rare."

Oddly, Angie didn't ask him why there was only one room key. In fact, it didn't seem to register with her at all. They entered the room and he tossed their bags on a chair, while she put the empty case in the closet. "It's risky either way, but I think it'll be safer here than in the car," she said. The bag with the Gibson log book was still over her shoulder.

"Give me a second to freshen up, and we'll go downstairs to meet Dusty," she said.

"This has not been a typical day at the office," he smiled to himself as he walked to the window. From the room's window he could see the parking lot nearly filled with dealer vans and trucks.

"Okay, ready," said Angie a few minutes later. She had added some eyeliner and lipstick. Ben noted that evening Angie was a little bit fancier than daytime Angie. He liked them both.

With Angie still carrying the log book, they took the elevator back down to the lobby and entered the bar. Dusty was already there, at a high-top table with a Coke in his hand.

"What's up with the drink?" Angie asked, pointing to the Coke.

"I'm off the hard stuff now," he said. "Those old days of ours took their toll."

"Come on," she said, "We weren't that bad."

"I might have taken it a step or two further when you weren't around," he said. "But all is good now. So, back to the guitar…"

"It's a 50s Gibson that belongs to Ben's aunt," said Angie. "Some traveling shyster conned her out of it.

"We don't have a lot to go on," she continued. "But the guy we're looking for bragged that he owns a guitar that used to belong to Elvis."

"Hmmm. That doesn't ring a bell with me. But if he has anything to do with Elvis, Rob will know him!"

"Rob! That's right!" exclaimed Angie, "How could I have forgotten?"

She turned to Ben and said, "Rob is an Elvis fanatic. For his 50th birthday he had a giant Elvis face tattooed on his chest! If a guy at this show is bragging about Elvis, Rob will know him!"

From behind them they heard a voice, "Talking about me again, Angie?"

Chapter Twenty-One

He had never been distracted by another man's chest before.

But as Rob, Dusty and Angie sat around the table, laughing and reminiscing about guitar shows and deals they'd made, Ben couldn't keep his eyes off the drawing of a pompadour peeking out above the top button of Rob's shirt.

He was curious about the rest of the picture, but he wasn't sure if he wanted to see a 60-year-old man's chest while sitting in a bar in Valley Forge, PA. Even if that chest did feature a larger-than-life-size tattoo of Elvis Presley.

Glancing around the bar, he saw that the tables were filling with other vintage guitar dealers. The average age appeared to be in the mid-60s. The average hair color was thinning grey. Ben could see how Angie would stand out in this crowd. No wonder everyone seemed to know her.

Finally he heard the conversation turn to the missing guitar search.

"So, do you know anyone who claims to have an Elvis guitar?" Dusty asked.

"Signed by Elvis?"

"No. Owned by Elvis," said Angie.

"Hmmmm…" said Rob, scratching his chin. "As a matter of fact, I think I do. He does walk-throughs."

"Walk-throughs?" asked Ben, finally speaking up.

Turning to him, Rob replied, "Yeah. Guitar show booths are pretty expensive and some folks don't want to spend the money. So, they buy a ticket at the door, and walk their guitars around one or two at a time. It's not a problem; the promoters encourage folks to bring guitars to sell. They even give a discount on the admission if you're carrying an instrument. So, the walk-through sellers are welcome."

He continued, "I remember talking to a guy at the Columbus show. He kept insisting that he had Elvis's second D-18."

"I didn't know Elvis had two D-18s," said Dusty. "I know he had the one with the stick-on *Elvis* letters. But I thought he traded that in on the D-28. The one with the engraved leather cover."

"I've seen the famous picture," Ben said. "It's on the front of his first album. I always wondered if that covering would affect the sound?"

"Sure would," said Rob. "Once you put a heavy leather cover over an acoustic guitar it kills the volume. And the tone. It pretty much becomes a prop."

Addressing Dusty's question, Rob said, "You're right about the first D-18, the one with the stick-on letters spelling 'Elvis.' He used that from June 1954 until December 1954, when he traded it in on the D-28. But sometime in January 1955 he picked up a new D-18 to carry as a backup for the leather-covered D-28. He didn't use it very often…"

"Maybe on the gigs where he wanted people to actually hear him play!" Angie interrupted.

"Yeah," laughed Rob. "His second D-18 is not well known, but there are a handful of photos of him using it between January and April 1955. After that, it disappeared. And this guy you're looking for… I think his name is Mike… claims to have it."

"And does he?" asked Ben.

"He showed me some photos. He does have an old D-18. But the tortoise shell pattern on the pickguard doesn't match the one on Elvis's guitar. I think he's trying to pull something. He seemed a bit shady."

"So far, he's sounding like our man," said Angie. "This guy conned an old lady."

"That's pretty bad. What guitar did he get from her?" Rob asked.

117

Just as Ben was about to answer, Angie cut him off. "A family heirloom," she said, "We'll tell you more about it when we get it back."

"A mystery, huh Angie?" Rob said. "Well, if I can help, let me know."

"Just point him out if you see him tomorrow," she said.

"Will do," he said, as he stood up to leave. "Nice to meet you, Ben. And great to see you again, Angie."

Dusty spoke up, "I've gotta grab some grub. The pulled pork here isn't as good as Jack's in Nashville, but it's not bad. I'll be right over here if ya need me," he said, pointing to a nearby table.

Turning to go, Dusty said with a smile, "I'm keeping an eye on you, Ben."

As Rob and Dusty left the table, Angie leaned in close to Ben, "Let's not mention the Moderne to anyone yet."

"That's such a weird name," he said, pronouncing it slowly in two syllables, "Moe – dern. And your theory is that the word 'Moderne' is a misinterpretation of 'Modern 3'?"

"Well, now that I've read this," she said, patting the book safely hidden in her shoulder bag. "I believe that the guy who originally listed the guitar in this book in 1958… or maybe someone who saw the listing… made a note about a 'Modern 3' guitar. Years later, in the early 1970s, the '3' was misread as an 'e.' And we ended up with 'Moderne.'

"Remember, Gibson originally only patented the shapes, not the names, of those three guitars in the Modernistic series. Two of them were eventually called the 'Flying V' and the 'Explorer.' But the third guitar, the one sketched by Red Brown, never had an official name. That is, until vintage guitar collectors came up with one years later. The 'Moderne.' And that's how even Gibson refers to it now."

"Really?" asked Ben, "The name didn't come from Gibson?"

"Nope. But that's not unusual. Guitar companies often adopt terms coined by the vintage community. 'Spaghetti logo,' for example. Today the Fender logo is bold and easy to read, but it originally featured thin flowing letters. In the mid-1970s a guitar dealer in Washington wanted a shortcut to distinguish his older Strats from newer ones. He humorously thought that the original Fender logo looked like it was written with spaghetti, so he started to refer to the older instruments as 'Spaghetti Logo' guitars. The term stuck, and now even Fender uses it.

"Likewise with the term, 'Slab Board.' Fender started to install rosewood fingerboards on their guitars in 1959. Years later, as the vintage market developed, collectors noticed that in late 1962 Fender switched to a thinner piece of rosewood on the fingerboard. Those original guitars made between 1959 and 1962, with the thicker slab of rosewood, became known as 'Slab Boards.' So, if someone says they have a 'Slab Board Tele,' you'll know it's from `59 to mid-`62."

She then laughed to herself, as she remembered another example. Turning to Dusty who was sitting two tables away, she said, "What was that you always said about non-vibrato Strats?"

He looked up from his dinner, smiled, and said, "Hard-tail, hard sale!"

"Thanks babe," she said laughing.

Looking back at Ben she said, "Most Strats have a vibrato bridge. But since 1955 Fender has also offered a non-vibrato option. Collectors eventually started to call the non-vibrato Strats, the ones with fixed bridges, 'Hard-tails.' Now Fender uses the term, too.

"Anyway," she continued, "Those are just Fender examples, but you get the idea. Collectors and dealers come up with new terms, and many of those terms make their way into the vintage guitar lexicon. So when the rest of the world started using Moderne as the name of the mystery third guitar from the Modernistic Series, Gibson went along with it."

"And has anyone ever seen one?"

"Well. They've seen an approximation. In 1982 Gibson re-issued it. Kinda…"

"Kinda?" he laughed.

"Do you remember that L-6S we saw in Harrisburg?" Angie asked.

"The copy that was so good it fooled your friend at the pawn shop?" he said.

"Right. In the mid-1970s the Fujigen Gakki company in Japan decided to step up their game and produce copies of American guitars that were equal to or better than the US-made originals. And in 1975, under their Ibanez brand, they really got everyone's attention with three unusual new instruments. Guitars that not even Gibson was making: Replicas of the three Modernistic guitars. Many people consider these three Ibanez guitars to be the first ever 'Vintage Reissues.'

"Fujigen obtained an original 1958 Flying V and Explorer to copy. And their reissue versions, called the Rocket Roll and The Destroyer, were impressively accurate even down to the Korina wood bodies.

"For the third guitar, though, there was no original to work from. So Fujigen used Gibson's patent drawing as reference. The only problem is that the patent drawing doesn't indicate the position of the knobs, the selector switch, or the shape of the pickguard. Fujigen had to guess. They ended up with a pickguard that covered most of the face of the guitar."

"What did they call that model?" Ben asked.

"They used a name that Gibson originally considered for the Explorer, The Futura."

"And let me guess what happened," asked Ben, "After Gibson saw the Ibanez reissues, they figured that they'd better make their own?"

"100% correct! Although, first they sued. *Then* they started on their versions. Gibson finally had their three Modernistic reissues ready by 1982. They called them the Heritage Series."

120

"And is that when Gibson started using the Moderne name?"

"Correct again! You're getting good at this. Since the rest of the world was already calling the mystery third guitar the 'Moderne,' Gibson officially went with that. Just like Ibanez, though, they had to guess with the pickguard, the knobs and the switch. Gibson decided to use a much smaller pickguard than the Ibanez version."

"So, if we find this Mike guy, and Red Brown's guitar…" Ben said, nodding to Angie to finish the sentence.

"Right! We will be changing the vintage guitar world. Starting with the pickguard." she said excitedly.

Suddenly Dusty pulled up a chair. "Y'all are gabbin' up a storm over here! Mind if I join in?"

"Not at all, Dusty," said Angie. "Ben is fascinated with the history of the guitar, so let's pick a brand and start teachin'."

Angie gave Ben a wink, indicating that the Moderne lesson was done for the evening.

For the next hour Angie, Dusty and Ben shared laughs, drinks, bar food, and, as Dusty pronounced it, 'git-ar' stories.

***

Finally, after a long day for everyone, the bar started to clear out. As Angie and Ben rode the elevator to the third floor, she said, "You were lucky to find a room in the hotel. I thought it'd be sold out."

"Sharing the room won't be a problem, will it?" he asked.

"Not for me," she said. Laughing, she added, "I can always stand the empty Moderne case between the beds for protection, if I have to."

Fifteen minutes later they were both snug in their respective beds. As Ben started to doze off he could see Angie reading a copy of a guitar magazine she picked up in the bar.

"All of this talk about guitars almost makes me wish I was back in the business," she said. "Almost."

Chapter Twenty-Two

Even in his groggy, half-asleep state, Ben appreciated waking up to the sight of a pretty woman.

"Time to get up, sleepyhead!" said Angie, already dressed and ready to go.

Ben's head rattled, as he tried to put the long day in perspective. But there was little time for reflection.

"What time does the show open?" he asked.

"It opens to the public at 10 am," said Angie, "But the doors open for the dealers at 9. I thought you might like to look around a bit, before we go in search of our man."

By 8:55 am they were standing in a long line of guitar dealers, waiting for the Expo Center doors to open.

"Let me get this straight…" he said to Angie, as he sipped the coffee he had picked up on their way out of the hotel. "The guitar show doesn't officially open to the public until 10 and the booths were set up yesterday. But all of these dealers are here, lined up and waiting, to get in an hour earlier? Just so they can spend more time looking at guitars?"

"Yep, that's exactly it," she replied.

Ben tried to imagine his co-workers at Bismark Insurance showing up for work an hour early…voluntarily. No, he thought to himself, that would never happen.

At the stroke of 9:00 the doors opened and dealers flooded into the large hall. Ben was amazed at the sheer number of guitars on display. Every possible brand and color.

Slowly he and Angie walked from one booth to another. At least 75% of the dealers they encountered stopped to say hello to Angie. Ben learned many of their stories. One was a college professor. One had spent time in India and scaled the Himalayas. One dealt in vintage cars as well as guitars. He was surprised to find that less than half owned retail stores. Many sold guitars out of their homes, or only at shows. Apparently that's what Angie used to do.

But one thing all of the dealers shared was a passion for the guitar. Oddly, that was what he most questioned in Angie. She knew as many details as any of them. And she was truly interested in guitars and their values. But Ben didn't see the pure joy that he saw in the eyes of many of the other dealers.

At one table they found a 1966 Gretsch Country Gentleman. Ben remembered seeing George Harrison use that model, and he had always been curious about it. It was so much bigger than the Melody Maker Ben played in his band in the 1970s.

"Wow, that's cool. Just like George's," he said, "Would it be okay if I tried it?"

Except for Ben and Angie, the booth was empty. The dealer who owned the guitars was out looking at other folk's stuff.

"Of course," said Angie, "But if you're thinking of buying it, check the binding first."

Confused by her comment, he picked up the guitar, and looked at the binding.

"Do you mean these brown spots?" he asked. "They don't seem like a problem…"

"Maybe not now," she replied, "But they will be."

"What do you mean?"

"In the early to mid-1960s Gretsch used an animal hide glue to attach the binding," she explained. "Now, fifty years later, the binding is reacting to the glue, and deteriorating from the inside out. No one seems to exactly understand the chemical process, but the result is a breakdown in the plastic binding. First brown spots appear, then cracks, then the binding turns to dust and flakes off. And since it starts on the inside, under the binding, there seems to be no way to stop it."

"Wow. Can you have it fixed?"

"Well," she said, "You can have the guitar re-bound. But that's difficult and expensive. They say that if you leave the guitar out of the case, the deterioration slows down. Perhaps the interaction of the glue and binding creates fumes, which are stronger when the guitar is sealed in the case. There may be some truth to that, because some of the worst examples I've seen have been on mint condition guitars that spent most of their time locked away in their cases. Some scientist somewhere should work on this problem. It's really had a negative effect on the value of vintage Gretsch guitars."

"I guess I'll put this one down," said Ben as he carefully put the guitar back on its stand.

"Sorry. I didn't mean to ruin your Beatle experience there…"

As they moved on to the next booth, they ran into Dusty.

"Angie, what's the price on that old Martin you left under my table?"

"Not for sale, Dusty. I'm going to take it home and learn how to play. By the way, are there any cool Beatle guitars here today? Ben wanted to see some."

That hadn't actually been Ben's goal, but he appreciated her efforts to entertain him. In truth, Ben was having a great time just being around so many different guitars. And Angie's commentary added to his enjoyment.

"Try Keith's booth, two rows over," Dusty said, "I don't know what he has with him, but he'll definitely talk your ear off about The Beatles."

"Thanks Dusty. I'll be back for the Martin later," she said.

Angie and Ben continued their stroll, passing table after table of classic old instruments. Since Ben's first visit to Pittsburgh Guitars, when they informed him that Aunt Maggie's old Strat was worth more than $20,000, he was in a constant state of sticker shock. But he wasn't prepared for the price tag on a 1959 Gibson Les Paul. As they approached the next booth he could see a faded sunburst Les Paul, displayed laying in its case rather than in a guitar stand. And right next to the handwritten "Please Do Not Touch" sign was a price tag of $245,000. Once again, the guitar's owner was nowhere to be seen. These vintage guitar dealers clearly had some sort of bond or trust among themselves. Which explained Angie's outrage that someone would pose as a dealer and attempt to steal Red Brown's guitar.

Two aisles over, as Dusty predicted, they found Keith. He was sitting at his booth, strumming a small black Rickenbacker. Like the other dealers he had grey hair but he wore it in more of a 1960s style with bangs.

"Hey Keith," said Angie. "Any Beatle stuff?"

"Just a couple of Ricks, and a blade-pickup Hofner," he said.

"Blade pickup?" asked Ben.

"Yeah, the `67 right over there," Keith said, pointing to a violin-shaped Hofner bass in the corner of his booth.

"Nice," said Ben. "It looks just like McCartney's."

Keith smiled. "Well, kind of...but not really. Different pickups. See that steel bar across the center of the pickup?"

"Is that what you mean by 'blade'? So, it's *not* the same as Paul's?"

"Pull up a chair," said Keith, pointing to two empty folding chairs.

Always ready to hear a guitar story, Ben reached for the chairs. Rather than sit down, though, Angie said, "If you don't mind, I'm going to look for Rob. I want to be ready if you-know-who shows up."

Turning to Keith, she nodded toward Ben and said, "You better start at the beginning..."

126

Ben smiled, and then, looking at Keith, he asked, "When is the beginning?"

"February 9, 1964," said Keith. "The Beatles first appearance on Ed Sullivan. That night is significant on many levels. First of all, most of the country fell in love with the band, so that assured their career success in the USA. At least for the foreseeable future. Secondly, an entire generation of kids were inspired to learn to play guitar. So every instrument manufacturer benefited. They were selling guitars as fast as they could make them.

"But there was one other interesting facet of the evening, one that most people miss. That night was one of the oddest musical instrument promotional events ever! Here was a band in an extremely high-profile situation, where millions of kids were watching their every move. And *none* of the three guitars they were playing were available for sale in the versions used by the band.

"Paul's bass, the Model 500/1, was made in 1963. But by the time Paul made it to the Ed Sullivan stage in `64, Hofner had changed the logo on the headstock to raised plastic letters and they added white binding to the neck. And by the time they started shipping large numbers of the bass to the US to satisfy the demand, they had changed the way the pickups were mounted.

"George's Country Gentleman was also made in 1963. But by 1964 Gretsch changed the pickup configuration, putting a different pickup in the neck position. Shortly after that they changed the style of the machine heads.

"And with Rickenbacker... well, that's just a confusing mess all the way around. John's original 1958 Rickenbacker 325, the one he used on the first *Ed Sullivan Show*, had a solid top on it. But by 1964 Rickenbacker only made that model with an f-hole, instead of a solid top. Just the same, right before the show they gave him a brand new guitar with a solid top. So on the second *Ed Sullivan Show* a week later, John was using a brand new Rickenbacker guitar that Rickenbacker no longer made. If you ordered a Rick 325 the day after the Sullivan show, you'd get one with an f-hole, not a solid top like John's."

"Wow," said Ben, trying to remember John Lennon's guitar.

Keith continued, "And Rickenbacker continued this craziness with George! While The Beatles were in New York for *Sullivan*, Rickenbacker gave George a brand new Rick 12-string. He liked it so much he immediately started using it on hit records. And it was prominently used in the *Hard Day's Night* movie released later that summer. So, what did Rickenbacker do, as that 12-string became internationally famous? They immediately changed the design of the guitar!

"If you rushed out to order a Rickenbacker 12-string the moment you first saw a picture of George Harrison playing it, you'd end up with a different guitar."

"That's amazing," said Ben. "How could these companies be so foolish?"

"Well," said Keith, "In their defense, they didn't see The Beatles coming. All of these companies had been making instruments for a long time. And along the way they continually made modifications, sometimes to improve the instrument, sometimes just stylistically. They never anticipated a sudden worldwide demand for specific models."

"So did they immediately revert to the versions that The Beatles were using?" Ben asked.

"Nope. Gretsch, Rickenbacker and Hofner were hit with more orders than they could possibly fill. There was no motivation for them to make guitars exactly like the ones used by The Beatles. Sure, some kids were disappointed. But for the most part, no one knew any better."

"That's too bad," said Ben.

"I used to think that way, too," said Keith, "But you have to step back and look at the big picture."

"How's that?"

"The day after The Beatles appeared on TV, every kid in America wanted to play guitar. A good percentage of them bought a guitar…or rather, had their parents buy them a guitar. A certain percentage…I don't know, maybe half…actually tried to learn how to play. And a percentage of *those* kids learned well enough to form a band. And a percentage of *that* group stuck with it to become musicians.

"Meanwhile, while all of that was happening, a very small group of individuals spent enough time studying photos to notice that the Rick 325 John is holding on the cover of *The Beatles Second Album* was not the same as the guitar available in stores. These folks noticed that the Hofner Bass you could buy in the USA had blade-pickups, like that one over there, rather than the pickups on Paul's bass.

"The slight differences between The Beatles' guitars and those played by everyone else in the world was fascinating to this small group of people. They needed to solve the puzzle. And it inspired them to learn more about not only those guitars, but *all* guitars. Once you learn that in 1964 Gretsch changed the little round piece of material under their mute switch from red felt to black felt, you're hooked. You want to know when the Les Paul Special went from a single cutaway to a double cutaway. Or when Fender added a second string tree to their headstocks. Have you noticed that most of the dealers here are the same age?"

Looking around, Ben said, "Now that you mention it…"

Keith continued, "These guys got into the business of buying and selling guitars at different times. But the root of their passion goes back to the 1960s. That's when the fascination started. That's when it worked its way into their souls. Not all of them will trace it back to The Beatles

129

on Ed Sullivan. But more than you would guess. And if not The Beatles, then some other band they saw as a kid."

"And," Ben said, understanding Keith's point, "There's nothing like a mystery and a quest to draw you into a subject!"

"Right," said Keith. "I was just a kid who wondered why George Harrison's Rick-12 had squared-off edges with binding and Roger McGuinn's Rick-12 in The Byrds had rounded front edges." Motioning around the room, he added, "We're all here today because at some time in our life we embarked on a search for a particular model, or color, or year of some guitar. And that search led us to the world of vintage guitars. And what an interesting world it is!"

Looking over to the front door of the room, Keith said, "It looks like they're letting the public in. I better straighten up the booth. Nice talking to you."

"Yeah! Thanks!" said Ben.

Just then he felt a tug on his sleeve.

"Ben," Angie whispered, "Rob says he sees our guy. And I've got a plan."

Chapter Twenty-Three

"Have you had any experience with confrontations?" Angie asked as they hurriedly made their way through the mass of Expo Center visitors.

"I've negotiated some pretty heated insurance contract mergers," said Ben, trying to keep up.

"Good," said Angie, "Get ready to put on your stern face. But not just yet."

They stopped at Dusty's booth and moved close to the tables, allowing the steady stream of guitar fans to move smoothly by them. She reached over and unpinned Ben's Dealer badge, putting it in her pocket and then did the same with hers.

"Here's the plan," she said. "Early in the show like this, if you stop in the middle of the aisle, it's easy to block the flow of traffic. That's what we're going to do. See Rob over there?"

Ben looked up and saw Rob one row over to their left. Ben smiled and waved. Rob smiled and waved back.

"Don't wave!" Angie said, pulling his arm down.

"Rob is going to text me when he sees our guy heading down this aisle," she said. "We're going to casually step out into the middle of the aisle, so the guy we're looking for will get stuck in the crowd...and he'll overhear our conversation."

"Okay. But why?" Ben asked.

"First we have to make sure that this is the guy who stole Red Brown's guitar. Then we have to get him out of this crowd so we can get tough with him," she replied.

"I presume you mean get tough *verbally*?" Ben asked.

131

"I'll make that decision when I see how tall he is," she said, temporarily smiling.

"Just follow my lead," she continued, "This guy thinks he's an Elvis expert. And he thinks he has an Elvis guitar. So, let's tempt him with another one. I talked to Rob and he said that Elvis's first good guitar was a Martin 000-18. Elvis used it on a few of his Sun recordings before moving on to the bigger D-18. And today no one knows the whereabouts of that 000-18."

"I'm with you so far…" said Ben.

"Well, what if *we* have that guitar?" she said, "What if your Aunt Maggie got her 000-18 in late 1954, at the same time Elvis sold his."

"Aunt Maggie has Elvis's guitar?!" he asked, facetiously.

"No," she said, lightheartedly pushing his shoulder. Then, looking him in the eye and smiling, she added, "But she *could…*"

Ben smiled back.

"Look," she said, "We just need to get him to stop and talk to us. If we find out that he's our guy, then we'll work him over."

"You mean work him over *verbally*, right?"

She laughed. "Just play along, okay?"

A moment later her phone buzzed. She looked down at the text: 'Red shirt, blue Martin case.'

She looked back at Ben and added, "Oh, and pretend she's *my* Aunt Maggie…"

Angie grabbed Ben's elbow and they slowly worked their way out into the middle of the aisle. As she saw the guy in the red shirt approaching she whispered to Ben, "Ask me about the guitar."

Ben had never been a part of an improv group before, but the last few days had been full of new experiences. He may as well try this, too.

As he and Angie stood in the middle of a crowd of guitar enthusiasts, he said, "So you think your Aunt has Elvis's guitar?"

"Yeah," she said, looking back at him, "She tells me she got it in 1955."

She continued her story, "It has a letter 'V' stuck on it. But I told Maggie it couldn't really be Elvis's. I guess there's no way to know."

Just as Angie predicted, the guy in the red shirt had trouble maneuvering around them, especially while carrying a full-size guitar case in the crowd. And when he heard the name "Elvis" he stopped to listen to the conversation.

He turned toward Angie, and without introducing himself, interrupted them. He had short grey hair that stuck up in the front, a thin stringy moustache, and old-fashioned glasses that looked like they belonged on a high school teacher in the 1950s. In a not particularly friendly tone he said, "You have an Elvis guitar?"

"Well, we're not sure," she replied. "My Aunt Maggie said she got it in 1955."

"Where is it?" he asked.

"A couple of hours north of here," she said, as innocently as she could. "In Bethlehem. Do you know where that is?"

"Yeah, I just got a guitar there a little over a month ago."

"Oh," said Angie as she looked over and locked eyes with Ben. They both knew this was their guy.

He continued, "Where does your aunt live? Can I see the guitar?"

Still in her acting mode, Angie said, "Oh, wow, it would be great if you could check it out for us! I have some photos of it on my web site…"

She then tapped several times on the screen of her phone. Ben could see that the taps were random.

Looking back at the red shirted guy, she said, "I can't get any signal here in the convention center. Let's go outside. I'll be able to log on out there."

Without waiting for an answer she started to walk toward the door. Ben and the guy followed obediently behind.

They passed the guard taking tickets at the door, and then walked down the hallway toward the check-in desk. Across from the check-in desk, near the front door of the building, was a small, unused conference room.

Seeing that room, Angie said, "This is close enough to the front. Let's try in here."

She confidently entered the room, still poking at her cell phone screen. Entering the room seemed to be an odd choice to the red shirted guy, but his greed for the Elvis guitar over-rode any hesitation. He followed Angie in, with Ben right behind him.

The click of the closing door startled him, but before he could say anything to Ben, Angie spoke up.

"Look, Mike …or should I say Mick," she said, sliding the fake receipt he gave to Mrs. Brown across the conference table.

His eyes widened.

She continued, "There is no Elvis Martin. We're here for the guitar you stole from our friend."

He turned toward the door, but saw Ben standing there. Conjuring up memories of difficult business meetings in the past, Ben adopted his 'stern face.' He was pleased with the apparent results.

Mike turned back toward Angie. "I don't know anyone in Bethlehem. I've never even been there," he lied.

Ben decided to really get into the spirit of the event. Taking a step toward Mike he said, "Listen buddy, you didn't get a chance to meet Mrs. Brown's grandson, Jason. But he's a cop. And he has cameras all around her house. We have lots of pictures of your smiling face."

Ben even shocked himself with his improvisation skills. He had to hold back a self-congratulatory smile. Instead he added, "Jason and his police friends will be happy that we found you."

Panic spread across Mike's formerly confident face.

"Hey, you guys," he said, "I was going to take her the money this weekend."

"The money?" Angie said, almost yelling.

"Yeah, yeah," he stammered. "It was a decent re-pro. The pickguard design was way off, but I got $3,000 for it. I thought that was pretty good. Here, I'll give you money now. $3,000 minus my 20% is $2,400."

He reached into his pocket and pulled out a roll of hundreds. He started to count out $2,400.

"You sold it?" said Ben, "That guitar is…"

Before he could finish, Angie interrupted with, "Very important to the family. Who did you sell it to?"

Mike's head was moving back and forth, as he listened to Angie on one side of him and Ben on the other.

"Where is it now?" Ben asked.

"Who has it?" asked Angie.

Flustered, he replied, "I took it to the Long Island Show. I sold it to Michel."

"Michel?" questioned Ben.

"Yeah. He's a dealer from France. He has a store in Paris. I don't know his last name…"

"Is he here today?" Ben asked.

"I doubt it," said Mike. "I only see him a few times a year. He mostly comes to the Long Island Show and takes stuff back for his shop. Why is this so important? It was just a Moderne copy."

Clearly frustrated, Angie poked him in the arm, "It's important because you didn't have any right to sell it. And you're not taking 20%."

135

Ben started to say something, but Angie put her hand up to stop him.

She continued, "Give us $2,700. You keep 10%, and you're lucky to have that. You're lucky we're not having you arrested! And this Michel guy, he's short with dark hair and glasses, right?"

"Yeah. But that's all I know about him. I don't know the name of his store," he said as he handed Angie the money.

Angie grabbed the fake receipt and a pen that was laying on the table. She turned the paper over. "I'm writing this deal down. Let me see some ID."

He was anxious to leave the room, but Ben still blocked the exit. Reluctantly Mike handed Angie his license. She took a quick photo with her phone, and said, "Sign this receipt. And if we hear about you ripping off another old lady, we're coming after you."

Mike signed, grabbed the guitar he had been carrying, and hurried out the door.

Ben turned to Angie and said, "I'm surprised you let him keep $300."

"We need him to be out of this deal," she replied. "If we took all of the money, he'd be telling people we robbed him. As it is now, he's happy that he made a little bit of cash, and hopefully he won't be blabbing to everyone about it.

"Besides, $300 is nothing compared to what this guitar is worth."

They both stood in silence for a moment. Ben could feel his heartbeat slowing back down to normal levels.

"What now?" he asked.

"Follow me," she said, as she reached into her pocket for their badges. In a few minutes they were back at Dusty's booth.

"Dusty, babe," she said. "Give me $3,500 for that Martin."

"Can I at least look at it first?" he said, smiling.

"No," she said. "It's an 1874 1-28 and it's worth $5,000. At $3,500 it's a bargain."

"Well, I'm sure not gonna retire on this deal," he said, reaching into his pocket.

Taking the money, she leaned up and kissed him on the cheek. "Thanks, darlin'. We've gotta go. Please say 'Thanks' to Rob for me."

She turned, nodded at Ben as if to say, "Let's go," and motioned toward the door.

Ben, who had been standing there silently, looked at Dusty, smiled and shrugged.

Dusty smiled back, saying "Have fun, you guys."

As they made their way to the exit, Ben said, "I thought your Martin wasn't for sale?"

Still walking, she said, "We need money for airfare…"

He stopped in his tracks.

She stopped and turned toward him, "Come on, we have to get back to Pittsburgh, to get our passports. You do have a passport, don't you?"

Chapter Twenty-Four

Ben and Angie were traveling west on the Pennsylvania Turnpike, heading back to Pittsburgh. For the last 24 hours she had repeatedly told dealers at the Philadelphia guitar show that she wasn't interesting in parting with the Martin. Then, right after learning that Red Brown's missing guitar was in Europe, she quickly sold the Martin to her old dealer friend, Dusty.

After 20 minutes of silence Angie spoke up. "It was fun taking the guitar to the Martin factory," she said. "And it was nice to know that it was made over a century ago. But right now we have a better use for the money."

"But…" Ben didn't know which topic to address first. How could she be so cavalier about selling a rare old instrument? And were they really going to France?

Angie answered the second question before he could ask it. "Red Brown's guitar is very important. It's important to his family, and it's important to the vintage guitar world. We've lucked out so far. That thief Mike didn't know what he had. With no case and no paperwork, he foolishly presumed it was fake. But Michel, the French dealer he sold it to, is a lot smarter. He will eventually take it apart and examine the wiring and construction. He's going to figure it out. We have to get there before he does."

"So," asked Ben, stunned at the very concept of what he was about to ask, "Your plan is that we should drop everything and immediately fly to Paris?"

"Yes."

"But have you been to Paris? Do you know where we're going? How will we find the guitar and how will we get it back?" After a pause, he added, "And what about my job?"

Angie briefly glanced over to the passenger seat, and then back to the road. She was driving just a bit faster than Ben had driven when they headed east two days ago.

"How long have you been at your job?" she asked.

"35 years."

"And how often has there been a once-in-a-lifetime experience at work? Are you expecting one this week?"

"No," he said, as he considered the tedious daily routine at Bismark Insurance.

"Well then," she said, "Take a few more days off. They'll get by without you. Besides, you've already given them half of your life."

She was right. He had worked long and hard for the company. The real truth was that he *would* be missed at his meetings, but only until they found someone to replace him.

"Okay," he said, "I'm in."

"Good. Now, about your other questions, no, I haven't been to Paris. But I've been to the guitar shops on Denmark Street in London. I was there a few years ago making a trade. And just like in London, I believe most of the guitar shops in Paris are on the same street. I'm sure the store owners all know each other. Michel has been to many US guitar shows and he has taken a lot of guitars back to France. Someone will be able to point us in his direction. And, how will we get the guitar back? We'll cross that ocean when we come to it."

She looked over and smiled at him.

He smiled back. Her enthusiasm was infectious.

"Okay!" she laughed, "We're on our way!"

***

139

As the miles wore on, he pondered the expense of the upcoming travel. He had money in his savings account that could cover the cost. And it was his idea to drag Angie into this search in the first place. He again felt bad about her selling the old Martin.

"I'm sorry that you sold your guitar."

"Oh, don't worry about it," she said. "I still made some money on it."

"But what about its history? Didn't you want to keep it?"

"I have other guitars," she said.

"But that one was from 1874," he said, "And it was signed inside by the shop foreman..."

"Ben," she said, "There are two kinds of folks who have a lot of guitars, players and collectors. And I'm neither."

"But you used to have a lot of guitars. You bought and sold them for years. And I know you appreciate the instrument...it's the basis of rock and roll, the music of multiple generations. Didn't you ever want to keep some of those guitars? Didn't you ever feel an emotional attachment to them?"

"Let's not overly romanticize it," Angie replied. "Sure, the guitar is the sound of rock and roll. But the individual guitars are just the tools used to make that music. They're just tools. Would you have an emotional attachment to a shovel?"

"Maybe," he said. "I would if it was a crafted work of art, like a guitar. I admit I hadn't looked at my guitars in years. But spending these last two weeks seeing so many guitars, and talking about them with you, reminded me of the magic I felt when I was a kid... when I was twelve years old and my mother bought me the Melody Maker. When I played my first chord on that guitar I fell in love with it, and with music. It was me and that guitar... a team... facing the world.

140

"You've reminded me of that magic," he continued, "Now I want to learn everything I can about guitars…the models…the makers…"

"I'm glad you appreciate the instrument," she said, "But you have to remember, it's just an inanimate object. It's a product designed to be sold. Leo Fender didn't play guitar. He didn't set out to create a work of art. He just wanted to make the best guitar that he could, so he could sell it.

"And another guy, Nat Daniels. His goal with Danelectro was to make an inexpensive, yet reliable guitar. And he did. And along the way, he designed the first 12-string, the first six-string bass, the first electric sitar, the first tilt-adjustable neck, the first shielded electronics, and more. And did he play guitar? No. He was an inventor, not a guitar player. After he sold Danelectro he designed a boat.

"Many of the guitar manufacturers, Gretsch, Harmony, Kay, Fender and more, sold out to big corporations in the mid-1960s when the guitar boom was at its highest. And they sold their companies because they were in business to make money.

"Norlin was a South American beer company when they bought Gibson in 1969. And did they buy it for art? No, they bought it because Gibson was successful at selling Melody Makers to kids like you."

Ben was taken aback by Angie's attitude. But she didn't sway him.

"The motivation of the manufacturers isn't relevant," he countered. "Even if their primary goal was to make money, they still created art along the way. Leonardo Da Vinci was commissioned to paint the Mona Lisa. Did the amount he was being paid cross his mind as he was painting? Was he thinking, like the guitar makers you've mentioned, 'I better do a good job on this, so that I can make more money on the next one'? Who knows. But does it matter? In the end he created a work of art."

"I hope you're not comparing a 335 to the Mona Lisa," she said.

"Of course not," said Ben. "But a 335 *is* a work of art. And I think even Da Vinci would agree." He laughed, and added, "Well, at least he'd be impressed with concept of electricity."

Continuing, he said, "And to add another dimension, since it gives you the means to write and play music, a guitar is a work of art that enables you to create *more* art!"

Angie replied, "Look, I'm not trying to knock the inherent beauty of a well-made guitar. Maybe my lack of interest in stockpiling them is colored by the many times I've bought instruments from the estate of a late collector. People who spent their entire lives putting together some sort of collection of guitars...all from the same year, or all of the different finishes of a particular model, or whatever was important to them. And after they're gone, the family just wants to sell it. The family doesn't care about a unified theme. Or which guitars go with which other ones. They just want everything to be sold, and out of the way. You can collect whatever you want, but someday your family is going to sell it to someone like me, and it will be gone."

"You're missing the point," Ben said. "In fact, you're missing several points. First of all, this late collector that you're referring to had fun putting that collection together. It brought joy to his life. That alone made it worthwhile. Secondly, by compiling like instruments, he no doubt gained insight into certain details about those models. If he documented that, he had the opportunity to pass along information to future students of guitar history. Third, by collecting and protecting the guitars, he helped preserve them for future generations. And last, if you, the buyer, gave the family a fair price on those guitars, then they were able to benefit from the extra cash."

Angie was silent for a moment, as she thought about what he said. "That's an interesting argument, Ben."

"And another thing," he said smiling, "I think your lack of emotional attachment is partly due to the fact that you've never had the experience of playing music with other people. When we finish this Red Brown quest you and I are going to play guitar together. Maybe we'll form a band. I'm going to get you to stop viewing a guitar as 'product.'"

"Ha!" she said, "You haven't heard me play."

"You don't need to be great to have a good time playing music with your friends," he said. "Besides, Da Vinci wasn't that great when he started either. Have you seen his early work? It's mostly crayon."

She laughed out loud.

"Well, we'll be in Paris anyway," she said, "We can visit the Mona Lisa, and I'll try to view it as both art and a commissioned work. Then maybe I can start to understand guitars as emotionally as you do.

"And if Da Vinci's early work, the crayon era, is as bad as my guitar playing…then maybe I'll play with you."

Chapter Twenty-Five

"Close…but it's still good!" Ben said to himself.

It had been nearly ten years since he needed a passport, for a business trip to the Caribbean. When he finally found it among some old paperwork he was happy to see that it was still valid.

Moving on to the next task, Ben quickly checked Tripadvisor.com.

When he was driving the last leg of their return trip from the Philadelphia Guitar Show, Angie used her cell phone to book two tickets on the 7:25 pm flight to Charles De Gaulle International Airport in Paris. Ben told her that he would handle the hotel rooms.

With the passport search completed, he had just about an hour to shower, re-pack his bag, and book rooms in a city he knew little about. Some quick online research showed that many of the Parisian guitar stores were in an area called Pigalle. Further reading, though, indicated that the area was also known for its sex shops. He decided to look elsewhere in the city for a place to stay.

Then he flashed back to a Woody Allen movie he saw a few years ago, *Midnight In Paris*. The hero in the movie travels back in time to interact with American writers living in Paris in the 1920s. Those writers, including F. Scott Fitzgerald and Ernest Hemingway, met and drank in restaurants that are still active in Paris today, in the Saint-Germain-des-Pres district. Ben booked two rooms at The Artus Hotel, on Rue de Buci, half a block off of the area's main street, Saint Germain Boulevard.

Delta Flight 8573 would get them to Paris at 11:30 tomorrow morning, Saturday. Thinking ahead, he also booked a car to ride them from the airport to the Artus. If all went well, they'd have time to drop their bags at the hotel, freshen up, and make it Pigalle by mid-day. How they would find Red Brown's missing guitar was still a mystery. But Angie continually impressed him with her confidence and conviction. And at this point he'd follow her anywhere… even to Paris.

The flight was long, and uneventful. Ben watched two movies on the small screen built into the back of the seat in from of him. Although they both ate and napped on the plane, they were exhausted when they arrived at 11:30 am Paris-time. To their bodies it was 5:30 am.

The first sights along the 25-minute drive to the city were less than impressive… industrial areas, run-down neighborhoods, and office buildings. But when they entered Paris both Ben and Angie were struck by its beauty. The entire city had been redesigned and rebuilt between 1850 and 1870, and laws put in place at that time dictated a uniform look. Block after block they saw white stone buildings with a balcony on the third floor and another less-decorative one on the sixth floor. Wide boulevards connected monuments. And numerous beautiful stone bridges crossed the River Seine.

Plus, everywhere they looked they saw cafes with rows of small round tables on the sidewalk, each with two chairs positioned facing the street. Shoulder to shoulder folks sat sipping coffee or wine, watching life go by in front of them.

Ben was so taken by the scene, he turned to Angie and said, "It's *just* like in the movies."

"I can't believe it either," she replied. "It's what I pictured…but I didn't think it would be *exactly* what I pictured."

Turning on to Boulevard Saint Germain, the car in quick succession passed two of the cafes frequented by 1920's American writers, Café de Flore and Les Deux Magots ("I bet that's not pronounced the way it looks," whispered Ben). One block further, at yet another café, Café

Mabillion, the car turned on to a narrow side street, and delivered them to the Artus Hotel.

Checking in, they were given two rooms on the third floor. Ben was shocked at the size of the elevator. In the few minutes he had to read hotel reviews before leaving Pittsburgh, Ben noticed that many Americans commented on the small size of Parisian hotel rooms. He didn't think the miniaturization would start at the elevator.

"It's a good thing that we're friends," he said.

"And it's a good thing we only brought carry-on!" Angie laughed.

The elevator clearly would not have held two people plus two full-size suitcases.

When they arrived at the third floor, they saw that the small hallway only featured three rooms. Their rooms were directly across from each other, and so close that one person could turn both doorknobs at the same time.

"Welcome to Paris," Angie said with a smile.

"What's our plan now?" Ben asked. Looking at his phone he saw that it had already adjusted to local time. "It's now 12:45."

"I'll meet you in the lobby in an hour," she said. "We'll grab some coffee and find our way to Pigalle."

Ben's room had a small bed, a small desk, and a small closet. But just as the online reviews had predicted, the room was spotless and cheery. And the bathroom was surprisingly nice. "So far, so good," he thought.

An hour later the phone woke him from a deep sleep. He didn't even remember laying down, but apparently he had leaned back on the pillow and closed his eyes for what he thought was a minute.

"I'm pretty out of it, too," Angie said on the lobby phone. "But I exchanged some dollars for euros and got a subway map. It won't take long to get there. Come on down, and we'll get some lunch to boost our energy level."

Ben met her in front of the hotel, and they turned left down the side street, Rue de Buci. Just as they had seen on the main boulevard, every block contained at least one or two cafes. And every café had small, two-person tables facing outward on the sidewalk. They randomly picked one, Bar du Marché, and sat down. Ben greeted the waiter with his best *"Bonjour,"* and the waiter immediately replied, "I'll get the English menu."

They ordered sandwiches and coffee, and while they waited they saw a man across the street carrying a guitar case and a small battery-powered amp. He stopped, directly across from them, opened his guitar case on the sidewalk, plugged in his guitar and started to play. Almost immediately, folks gathered around him as he played a complex classical piece.

"Well, there's something you don't see every day," said Angie.

"You mean someone busking in the street?" said Ben. "We have those in America."

No," she replied, "I meant the guitar."

It was obviously a nylon string guitar, but Ben did notice two odd white pickguards…one on either side of the soundhole. Ben presumed the player had added those himself.

"It's just a classical guitar, isn't it?" he asked.

"Yes and no," said Angie.

She continued, "That's a rare early 1960s Gibson Flamenco 2."

"Not to be confused with the Flamenco 1?" Ben asked, smiling.

"There wasn't a Flamenco 1," she said, smiling back at him.

"Even if I wasn't delirious from a lack of sleep, I think I'd be confused by this one," Ben said, as the waiter delivered their coffee.

As he sipped his coffee, Ben attempted to say to Angie, "Please continue." But what really came out was, "Please…ahhh, that's the worst coffee I've ever had!"

Angie laughed, and continued anyway. "Flamenco music involves percussive tapping on the face of the guitar. Gibson marketed that guitar during the height of the folk era in the early and mid-1960s. It's basically a classical guitar, but with less bracing so it's louder. And it has those two pickguards so you won't damage it when you tap the top while playing."

"And the '2' part?" Ben asked, still making a face from the coffee.

"Gibson's classical guitar models were all numbered… the C-0, C-1, C-2, C-3, etc. The Flamenco guitar was modeled on the C-2 classical. So it was called the Flamenco 2. But it was the only Flamenco-style guitar that Gibson made."

"Now that I look at it, it seems a little familiar," he said.

"It should," she said, sipping her coffee for the first time, "It's in that 1966 Gibson catalog you have. It's right at the end of the classical section. And you're right, this coffee is terrible!'

"My mother almost bought me a classical for my first guitar," said Ben. "The guy at the piano store in the mall told her it would be easier on my fingers."

"Did he mention that the neck would be twice as fat as the neck on an electric guitar? And it would be much harder to play?" said Angie. "And it would go out of tune faster?"

"And I couldn't *rock* on it!" Ben added, laughing. "No, he didn't mention any of that. But in her wisdom, my mother sensed that we should skip the piano store in the mall. She decided we'd be better off at an actual guitar store, like Victor J. Lawrence's. And she was right!"

"Speaking of guitar stores," said Angie, "Let's finish these sandwiches and get to the subway." Noticing the nearby signage, she corrected herself, "I mean the Metro."

"Bonjour!" said Ben.

"Bonjour?" she questioned.

"Hey," he said, "It's the only French I know!"

"Well, we may need more than that," Angie said. "We have a guitar to find."

Just then the guitarist across the street finished his song and the crowd around him broke into applause.

Hearing the clapping, Ben added, "See? Even people in the street are applauding our quest. What could go wrong?"

Chapter Twenty-Six

The subway, or the Metro as it is known in Paris, was easy to maneuver.

Unlike the New York City subway lines, which are labeled Uptown or Downtown, the Metro lines are distinguished by their end point. The train to Pigalle (Line 12 – Forest green on the Metro map), ends at Porte de la Chapelle, so Ben and Angie followed the signs in that direction.

Fifteen minutes later they were standing on a street corner in the Pigalle district. It was a busy, complicated intersection, with roads going off in all different directions. They were about to interrupt a passerby, when Ben noticed a long-haired guy carrying a guitar case down a side road.

"Let's follow him," he said, as they crossed the street and walked down a small hill on Rue Jean-Baptiste Pigalle.

As they passed several questionable looking bars, Ben turned and said, "I can't read the language, but I'm pretty sure I know what these places are offering."

"Some things are universal," Angie laughed.

At the next corner they found a mid-sized guitar shop. The owner was just opening a large expandable steel fence covering the front of the store.

"Désolé pour le retard, la pause déjeuner s'est un peu éternisée," he said as they approached.

Ben wondered why a shop would just be opening at 2:30 in the afternoon, but he was very fascinated with the selection of guitars in the window.

Seeing the look on his face, Angie whispered, "Those are all new reissues, you know…"

"Really?" he said. "But they look so old!"

"They beat up and relic new guitars these days, to make them look heavily played," she said. "And they're getting very good at it. At first glance it's hard to tell new from vintage anymore."

"I'll say," he said. In front of them was a Fender Custom Shop `53 Tele Reissue that looked exactly like an original 1953 guitar.

"But," she added, "There is still a certain vibe you get with an actual vintage guitar. Something you can kind of sense…"

She walked over to a 1963 Fender Jaguar. "The finish and hardware of a true vintage guitar have a patina that's hard to replicate. It can be done…so sometimes you simply have to take a guitar apart to verify its legitimacy. But after handling enough real ones you develop an intuition about it."

Between the strings of the Jaguar was a sign that read *"Occasion."*

"It must be a special occasion guitar," Ben said.

Overhearing the conversation, the store owner approached them.

"You are American?" he asked.

"Yes," said Angie. "I am Angie, and this is Ben. You have a beautiful store."

"Thank you," he said. "My name is Gregoire. Do you like the Jaguar?"

"Yes, but why does it say *'occasion'*?" asked Ben.

"O- cah- zee on?" Gregoire answered, pronouncing it correctly. "That means 'second-hand.' 'Used.'"

"I see," said Ben. "Do you mind if I ask another question?"

"No, not at all."

"Does your store only open at 2:30?"

151

"No," laughed Gregoire. "All of the guitar shops close from 1 until 2 for lunch. I was just running late. Don't the stores in America close for lunch?"

"Ha! No, they don't. But as soon as I get home I'm going to suggest it to Sam at my favorite guitar shop."

"By the way," Angie said, "We're looking for a vintage dealer named Michel. He brings guitars back from vintage shows in America."

"I'm sorry, I don't know him," Gregoire replied. "The only second-hand guitars I get are exchanges for new ones. But try 'Oldies Guitars.' They may know him."

He pointed to a shop a few doors down on the intersecting street.

"Merci," said Angie.

"Thank you," said Ben, shaking Gregoire's hand.

As they left the shop and turned onto Rue Victor Masse, Ben turned and said, *"Merci?"*

"Yeah," replied Angie, "I'm one ahead of you on French words."

He smiled as they walked.

Halfway down the block, on the right, they found Oldies Guitars. It was a much smaller shop, but at least 50% of the guitars were *'occasion.'*

"Bonjour, si je peux vous aider," said the owner, as they entered.

"Bonjour," said Angie. "Would you know a vintage dealer named Michel? He often visits America."

Ben was surprised that Angie didn't even ask if he spoke English. But, sure enough, the guitar store proprietor immediately replied.

"Oui. I see him from time to time. He sold me that guitar," he said, gesturing to a 1978 Strat hanging on the wall. "But I haven't seen him recently. He is more often at *Guitare Occasion.* Ask them." He pointed across the street and four doors down.

"Thank you very much," said Angie, as she reached over to the counter and took one of his business cards from a small display. "May I?" she asked.

"But of course!" he replied.

Looking at his card as they exited the shop, Angie turned to Ben and said, "Nice guy. Sorry we didn't have a chance to chat with him. But we're running out of time. And energy."

Ben nodded.

They were both surprised to see a bass guitar store immediately across the street. And next to it, a percussion store. It was certainly a musical neighborhood. But they both laughed when they saw the shop between the percussion store and *Guitare Occasion*. It had red velvet curtains and a neon sign that said, *'Le Sex!'*

Pointing at the sign, Ben laughed and said, "I'm really starting to pick up the language."

Guitare Occasion was about the same size as the first store they visited, but with twice as many guitars. And they were all vintage.

"There's some serious stuff in here," said Angie as they looked at a 1949 Gibson ES-175 in the window. "That's the first year for the 175. And that was Gibson's first guitar with a Florentine cutaway."

"Florentine?" asked Ben.

"A 'Florentine' is a sharp, cutaway versus a rounded one," she replied. "The rounded style is called a 'Venetian' cutaway."

She pointed at yet another valuable guitar in the window, a Gibson L-5 with a rounded cutaway.

"See that cutaway? Prior to World War II that was the only one Gibson used. But after the war they wanted to shake things up with something radical. So they introduced the sharp cutaway ES-175."

"Interesting," said Ben. "But, Florentine and Venetian? Florence and Venice are both in Italy. Were cutaway guitars invented there?"

"No," said Angie, "It actually has nothing to do with those cities. Gibson coined the terms years ago. Probably to make their guitars sound classier."

Two salesmen were in *Guitare Occasion*. One was standing next to a customer on the sales floor, and another sitting at a stool behind a small counter, looking at a computer screen. Since the customer was intently playing a Hofner bass, and the salesman looked completely bored, Angie approached him.

"Bonjour," she said.

The salesman looked at her without changing his expression. He obviously recognized her American accent. Without replying to Angie, he coldly turned to the guy behind the computer and said, *"Remi, peux-tu aider ces touristes?"*

Ben didn't know what was said, but he recognized the attitude.

Without looking up from the screen, the other salesman said, "How can I help you?" Though he clearly didn't care what their answer was.

Ben and Angie moved to the counter. They were both a little taken back by the first unfriendly Parisians they'd met.

Angie said, "Is Michel here?"

"No," he replied, still not looking up.

"Do you know when he'll be in?" she asked.

"No," he replied, "He's in America."

Angie took a step back and looked at Ben.

Behind them they heard the customer say, *"J'en ai déjà deux comme celle-ci. Tu n'as rien d'autre?"*

The salesman replied, *"Je vais voir,"* and then wandered off into a backroom.

Finally looking up at them, the guy behind the counter said, "Why do you want to see Michel?"

Ben stepped in and said, "We interested in buying one of the guitars he recently purchased in America." He looked at Angie as if to mentally confirm the model name. "It's a Moderne copy."

Looking back down at his computer screen, the salesman replied, "He sent that to us last week. It's already sold."

"Really?" Ben said dejectedly, not expecting an answer.

"Pardon," the first salesman said, as he squeezed by them with another Hofner Bass. He walked over and presented it to the customer still playing the first Hofner.

"Regarde-moi ce modèle! C'est de 1959," he said.

Angie couldn't follow the conversation, but she saw the customer wave him away saying, *"Non, non, j'en ai déjà, aussi!"*

"Qu'est-ce que tu cherches, au juste?" the salesman said.

"Quelque chose d'unique! Une Hofner hors gamme!" the customer replied.

Turning back to the guy behind the counter, Angie said, "Can you tell us who you sold the Moderne to?"

"Non, Madame, we cannot. That is confidential information."

Reaching for his wallet, Ben said, "We could make it worth your while…"

"Monsieur, we never reveal our clients! Our business is confidential" he said firmly.

Meanwhile, the conversation behind them was becoming heated. The salesman was obviously exasperated. He had shown the customer two vintage Hofners, but both were rejected. Yet Angie could see that the salesman did not want him to leave.

She suddenly had an idea. It was a long shot, but…

Angie moved in closer to the counter, and in a soft voice said, "Is that gentleman a Hofner collector?"

"It is not your business, but... *Oui,*" said the computer guy, intrigued by her question.

"And I bet he's a good customer. It would be nice to keep him happy."

Now he leaned in closer, and lowered his voice, "What do you mean?"

"If I could get you a rare Hofner," she said, "One that I know he doesn't have, would that make other information less *confidential*?"

He leaned back, put his hand up to his chin, and stared at her. He did not know what to think about this strange American.

Leaning back in, he quietly said, "What would you have?"

"In the early 1980s Hofner had a lot of extra parts laying around the factory," she said. "And in 1983 they offered a build-it-yourself kit. You'd get the bare wood parts, the electronics and a decal, and you could put it together and paint it yourself. They only sold a few. Most people have never even seen one."

He gave Angie a puzzled look. He wasn't sure if he believed her. Tilting his head towards the customer, he said, *"Jean-Luc, as-tu déja entendu parler d'un kit Hofner, où on batissait sa propre guitare?"*

They could both see the customer's eyes widen.

He turned back to Angie. "Bring it in and perhaps we can work something out."

"One minute please," she said, as she grabbed Ben's arm and headed out to the sidewalk.

She took out her phone and started dialing.

A few seconds later Ben heard her say, "Jeffrey, I know it's early in the morning, but I need a favor."

Ben remembered meeting Jeffrey at his pawn shop in Harrisburg.

"No, no, I'm out of town," she said. "Okay, okay, soon…"

Ben was only hearing half of the conversation, but he could tell that Jeffrey was asking her out.

"Remember that old Hofner Bass kit that was in the back room? In a box on the top shelf? Do you still have it?"

She nodded and smiled at Ben.

"How much?" Angie asked.

Not liking the answer, she said, "Come on, you've had it forever. There's probably fifteen years worth of dust on it!"

A second later she said, "Okay. Can you ship it for me?"

She continued, "Great. I'll get back to you later with the address. Thanks! Love ya!" And she hung up.

She looked at Ben and said, "He'll be surprised when he finds out he's shipping it to Paris."

Confused by almost every aspect of the half-conversation he just heard, especially the last two words, Ben followed her back inside.

She confidently walked up to the counter and said, "It's in America. It will be here in a week."

The man behind the counter was finally friendly. Obviously while she was outside making her call, he had made a preliminary deal on the Hofner build-it-yourself kit with the customer, Jean-Luc.

"Okay," he said, "I'll see you in a week!"

Angie leaned in closer and spoke softly again, "We need the Moderne info now. I'll make a deal with you. You pay the shipping from America, and I'll give you the Hofner Bass kit for free. You'll have it in a week, and you'll be able to sell it for big money to Jean-Luc."

"But I don't know you," he said, "How can I trust you that the kit will ever arrive?"

Angie looked down at the cluttered desk in front of him where she saw a copy of *Vintage Guitar* magazine. A monthly publication, *Vintage Guitar* features stories, interviews and articles about used and vintage instruments and contains ads from hundreds of guitar dealers around the world.

Pointing to the magazine, she said, "Is there anyone in *there* that you trust?"

"Of course," he said. "I have had dealings with Dan Daniels in Nashville."

Angie nodded. Daniels was the most well-known of all the vintage guitar dealers. He had been buying and selling old guitars for decades, before the term 'vintage guitar' even existed. He was an eccentric character but respected worldwide for his expertise.

"Let's call him," Angie said.

Looking at his watch, the salesman said, "His shop won't be open. It's only 8 in the morning over there."

After a few taps on her iPhone, Angie held it up for him to see. Her phone's screen was open to her Contact List.

"It's not a problem. I have his cell phone number. And he'll be awake. This is when he waters his flowers."

The salesman was speechless. He had clearly misjudged Angie.

Angie called the number.

"Hi, Dan. It's Angie. Sorry for calling so early, but I'm in Europe at a shop called *Guitare Occasion*… Yes… in Paris… Great. I'm making a deal here and they'd like to know if they can trust me. Would you mind speaking with them?... Thanks!"

She handed the phone over to the guy behind the counter. He was shocked at the turn of events.

"*Bonjour? Monsieur* Daniels?" he stammered.

The salesman recognized Dan's distinctive voice. "*Oui… oui… oui…*"

Angie recognized Dan's tendency to ramble on during a conversation.

Finally, the salesman said, *"Merci beaucoup,"* and handed the phone back to Angie.

"Thanks Dan," she said, "I'll see you soon… Yeah, I may be getting back in the business…maybe…OK, thanks…good luck with your roses."

She hung up the phone and looked back at the salesman.

Flustered, he reached beneath the counter and pulled out a box of receipts.

Shuffling through them, he said, "Ah… the Moderne."

Chapter Twenty-Seven

As Angie and Ben waited at the counter, the salesman shuffled through last week's paperwork.

"Ah, here it is," he said, showing them a receipt, "Gibson Moderne copy... sold for 4,000 euro."

Ben did some quick math in his head. He remembered that Mike, the unscrupulous guitar dealer who took the guitar from Mrs. Brown, sold the Moderne to Michel, a French dealer, for $3,000. He guessed that shipping the guitar to France would be at least another $200, increasing Michel's cost to $3,200.

Guitare Occasion sold the guitar for 4,000 euro, and Ben knew that one euro was worth approximately $1.20. But with only one hour sleep in the last 24, he was too groggy to do serious mental calculations. After years of handling financial situations back at Bismark Insurance, though, he couldn't help himself. He shook his head to rattle his brain cells, and multiplied 1.2 times 4 to get 4.8. So 1.2 times 4,000 is 4,800. In this case, $4,800. And $4,800 minus the $3,200 cost was $1,600.

Not bad, he thought. Michel and *Guitare Occasion* had made roughly $1,600 on a quick sale.

He then realized that he could have used the calculator in his phone for that process. "I am truly exhausted," he thought to himself.

As Ben was attempting to shock himself awake with math, Angie was staring at the receipt. The purchaser was listed as Madame Beauchamp, but there was no further identification.

The salesman turned the receipt away from Angie and stared at it for a moment.

"If I recall, it was a gift for the English gentleman accompanying her," he said.

Just then the phone rang. As he answered, Angie leaned in, straining to gather any other information from the receipt in his hand.

"Bonjour, Guitare Occasion," he said.

He smiled and continued the phone conversation, *"Ah, Michel. Il y des gens ici que voudraient savoir pour la Moderne..."*

But his countenance quickly changed. *"Mais elle est déjà vendue!"* he said.

Angie and Ben couldn't understand the subsequent discussion, but clearly Michel was calling from America. And he was not happy.

As he was speaking, the salesman opened a drawer behind the counter, slid the receipt in, and hurriedly closed the drawer.

"D'accord, je vais essayer de la trouver," he said, as he hung up the phone.

Turning to Ben and Angie, he said, "I'm sorry, I cannot help you."

"What's wrong?" Angie asked as innocently as she could.

"Michel thinks the guitar may have been real," he said, "He is upset with me for selling it before he returned. I cannot give you any information about the sale."

"What about our deal? The Hofner Bass kit in exchange for contact info?" said Angie.

"I cannot make that deal. Please leave now. I must find this guitar myself."

The salesman looked down at his desk and started rifling through papers.

"Au revoir," he said, without looking up.

***

"Well, that's not good," said Ben after they made their way out to the sidewalk.

"You're right," said Angie. "If one of these guys finds that guitar first it will disappear forever. But at least we have a name."

"Did you see it on the receipt?"

"Yeah. I'm not sure how you pronounce it here... 'Bow–shahm' maybe... Madame Beauchamp..."

"What do you mean, how you pronounce it here?" Ben asked.

"The name is important in the history of the electric guitar," she said, "But most people don't know it...or him, I should say. And that probably goes back to how the heck you say it."

"Sometimes you confuse me," Ben said, smiling.

"The name of the lady who bought the guitar is spelled B-E-A-U-C-H-A-M-P. And it's the same name as the man who invented the first practical electric guitar pickup. *That* guy started a company with Adolph Rickenbacker in 1931, and they made the first ever commercially produced electric guitar. His name was George Beauchamp, but he pronounced it 'Beech-um,' the way they pronounce that name in England.

"Adolph was a metal worker, a machinery guy. George was the technology guy. George not only invented the pickup, he also designed the shape of their guitar. But when it came time to eventually settle on a company name, they called it Rickenbacker."

"A name I *do* know," said Ben.

Angie continued, "And I think they chose Rickenbacker because it's easier to say than 'bo-sham' or 'beech-um' or whatever. Although, at the time they probably weren't thinking that the company would still be in business ninety years later. "

"Do you think George regretted not having his name on a successful guitar?" Ben asked.

162

"He died of a heart attack in 1941," she replied, "He didn't live to see the company in its heyday."

"For that matter," she added, "Adolph sold Rickenbacker in 1953, so he also wasn't part of the company when their coolest guitars were made. Although he lived until 1976, so at least he got to see John Lennon, George Harrison, and tons of other guys playing guitars with his name on them."

"I wonder how you would feel," said Ben, "If you started something... something with your name on it...and it became internationally famous after you were no longer involved. Would you be happy that everyone knew your name? Or sad that you weren't a part of the success?"

"Good point," said Angie.

As they both looked up and down the road, Ben said, "Well, what now?"

"We could try to look her up online," Angie said. "But I say let's start over there."

She pointed down the street to Oldies Guitars, the store they visited before *Guitare Occasion*. The owner of that shop had been kind and friendly.

As they crossed the street and walked a few doors down, she reached into her pocket and retrieved the business card she picked up earlier. The owner's name was on the card.

"*Bonjour*, Philippe," Angie said as they entered the store.

"Welcome back!" he said, smiling.

"Thank you for your help earlier," she said. "*Guitare Occasion* was the right place to find Michel."

Philippe nodded and said, "I am happy to be of service."

"I'm Angie, and this is Ben."

"*Bonjour Madame, Monsieur.*"

163

"I hope you don't mind another question?" Angie asked. "Do you know a woman named Madame Beauchamp?"

"No," he replied, "I'm sorry, that name is not familiar."

"She was in the neighborhood a week ago," said Angie, "Shopping for a guitar. With an Englishman."

"A lady with an Englishman?" he replied, glancing away, pondering the question. Then his eyes lit up, "Oh, yes, of course! She was here with Conor Kelly."

"Conor?" asked Ben. "Do you know him?"

"*Oui*," said Philippe. "Conor visits whenever his band is in town. He has never purchased a guitar from me, but he likes to stop in and look. He was here last week with a woman... one of his local fans."

"Did they say anything?" asked Angie.

"He asked if I had a Gibson Explorer. His friend back home has one and Conor wanted an exotic guitar like that. I told him that I was sorry that I did not have an Explorer, but even if I did, it would be expensive. I remember now that he nodded toward the lady he was with, and said that money would not be a problem."

"That's a pretty expensive gift to get from a fan," said Ben.

"She looked like she could afford it," said Philippe. "Maybe from her first husband? Perhaps the second?"

"Husbands?" asked Ben. "How old *are* these people?"

"Well, *monsieur*, I would never ask a lady how old she is, but Conor is near my age. Seventy-one or two, perhaps?"

"Please forgive me," Ben said apologetically. "When you said he was in town with his band, I presumed that Conor was young..."

"No, no, there are many older British bands who still tour in Europe," he replied. "There were thousands of bands in the 1960s and not everyone became as famous as The Beatles. Some of those musicians still play.

And they are great! And when bands come over from Liverpool, they still have many fans here in Paris."

"Did you say Liverpool?" asked Angie.

"Yes, Conor is from Liverpool. His band is called The Stormers. They may be older gentlemen, but they're an excellent band. They have a busy schedule."

"Do you think he's still in Paris?" Ben asked.

Phillipe replied, "I doubt it. They are generally only here for a week. He's probably back in England now."

Angie reached out to shake his hand. "You have been a tremendous help, Philippe."

"*Madame* is too kind," he replied, smiling.

As they prepared to leave, Angie turned back to Philippe. "Do you know a Hofner collector named Jean-Luc?" she asked

"Of course," he laughed, "Everyone does!"

She smiled back. "I will be sending you a package next week. You may not recognize what's inside, but it is 100% authentic, and Jean-Luc will pay a lot of money for it. It's a gift from me to you."

"I don't know what to say," he hesitantly replied.

"Well, don't say much, especially to your neighbors across the street. And tell Jean-Luc to keep it quiet too, if he wants to maintain good relations with everyone."

"Ha!" Philippe laughed, "A secret sale. Yes, we have done that with collectors."

"Good," she said. "And perhaps we will see you again."

"I certainly hope so," he said.

Once they were back out on the sidewalk, Ben said, "I think I can guess our next plan…"

As Angie pulled out her phone, she said, "Well, first I call Jeff, and tell him to send the Hofner bass kit to Oldies Guitars…"

"Then we go back to the hotel to sleep for a few hours…" Ben added.

"And *then*," she said, smiling, "We head to Liverpool!"

Ben laughed.

"Yeah, yeah, yeah, Angie!"

Chapter Twenty-Eight

Ben looked down at Angie's head resting on his shoulder and smiled.

Despite the jostle and rumble of the Paris Metro subway car, it was difficult for either of them to keep their eyes open. As Angie nodded off, Ben wished that he could join her. But his mind was racing. How could he possibly be in a foreign country, 4,000 miles from home, with a woman he barely knew, looking for a guitar he had never heard of? Where were they headed? And what about his job back home in Pittsburgh?

In his sleep-deprived state, he was losing his sense of perspective. So much had happened over the last few days. It was almost too much to grasp.

Ben shook his head in an effort to stay focused, and glanced around the subway car at his fellow travelers. Though they were headed to a variety of different destinations, he couldn't help but notice that even the most casually dressed Parisian had a certain artistic wardrobe flair. A scarf...interesting glasses...distinctive shoes...something to indicate that they *cared* what they were wearing. With his boring brown jacket, black jeans and sneakers, he felt out of place.

That's when he understood. Two weeks ago he was content to be negotiating insurance policies at his office desk. But recent events, which Angie seemed to handle as if they were everyday occurrences, had been a whirlwind of adventure. He realized that at this moment, in a subway car in Paris, he not only felt out of place in his clothes, he felt out of place in his life.

But unlike his fashion sense...was he the only person in Paris wearing sneakers?...he wasn't self-conscious about his quest with Angie.

His time with her had been far more interesting and exciting than anything he had experienced before. He decided it was time to embrace the adventure. For years he had heard the phrase "Life is short," but he never took it to heart... Starting today, he would. He was not going to waste one more moment worrying about the insurance company.

The last two weeks had been the most extraordinary days of his life. Almost beyond comprehension. As Ben recounted the events in his head, he still couldn't believe it all happened so fast. And he knew that if not for Angie, he'd still be sitting in Pittsburgh wondering what to do next. No. Worse. He wouldn't even have known there was a 'next.'

As he watched the Metro stations zoom by, he was happy that he remembered the name of their stop, Saint-Germain des Prés. On their way to the Metro from the guitar shops Angie had searched her phone for the best way to get to Liverpool. But doing that while walking, while trying to stay awake, proved to be difficult. He smiled at the sleeping Angie and decided that he would handle the next leg of their trip. He remembered seeing pictures of The Beatles at Pittsburgh Guitars and he could tell that they were big fans. He had a hunch that someone from Pittsburgh Guitars could direct them to Liverpool. As soon as he could figure out the time change between Pittsburgh and Paris, he would call the store.

At Saint-Germain des Prés he gently woke Angie and led her off of the subway car. She was a bit groggy as they walked up the stairs to the street level. They were both shocked when they reached the sidewalk and saw that the sun was still shining.

"Wow," she said, "What time do our bodies think it is?"

Looking at his phone, Ben replied, "It's really 4 pm. But my body thinks it's yesterday."

"It's only a couple of blocks to the hotel," he continued. "Let's try to stay up for a few hours, and I'll make some plans to leave town early tomorrow morning."

"What about the Mona Lisa? And the Eiffel Tower?" she asked.

"Do you want to see those now?" said Ben.

Holding back a yawn, she said, "No. We've got to get to merry old England. But next time."

He smiled.

"And," she continued, "Our return flight tickets leave from *here*, so next time will be soon!"

As they slowly walked back to the hotel, she put her arm through his.

All along the block, at cafés and restaurants, people were eating and drinking and chatting at little round sidewalk tables.

"It's a lovely city," she said.

"True," said Ben.

Surrounded by shoppers, romantic couples, and folks heading home for dinner with long loaves of bread, he added "And it's just like in the movies."

Among the crowds on the street, though, there was one thing Ben and Angie did not notice.

They were being followed.

Chapter Twenty-Nine

"Look, a table is open," said Ben.

They had reached Café Mabillion, on Boulevard Saint Germain.

He continued, "A croissant and maybe a glass of wine, *Madame*?"

"Spoken like a local," Angie interrupted, laughing.

"I know we're both about to crash," he said, "But the hotel is just around the corner. Let's stop here for a minute."

"OK," she said, as she slid into one of two chairs behind a small round table. There were two dozen such tables along the sidewalk in front of the café. And all of the chairs were positioned behind the tables, facing the street. People-watching was apparently an important part of the café experience.

As Ben joined her, a waiter walked by and said in a monotone voice, *"Bonjour. C'est pour boire ou pour manger?"*

When they both looked at him with confused expressions, he simply laid a menu on the table, turned and walked away.

Angie looked at Ben and laughed. "I don't believe they work for tips here in Paris. And… I think I'm getting giddy."

Ben smiled. In their sleep-deprivation state, he was holding up a little better than Angie.

He slid the menu to her and said, "You try to figure this out. I'm going to step over to the corner and call Pittsburgh Guitars. They'll be able to tell us how to get to Liverpool from here."

Ben walked to an open concrete area near the street corner.

Moments later Angie looked up to see a tall, grey-haired Frenchman standing at her table. With a heavy French accent he said, "Pardon me, miss. Can I help you translate the menu?"

Before she could reply, he sat down.

Reaching out to shake her hand, he said, "Hello, my name is Henri. Are you here in Paris for business or pleasure?"

She was surprised by his forward approach, but she could see Ben at the corner on the phone and she was surrounded by other café customers, so she was more entertained than concerned.

"Mostly business," she said.

"I see…" he replied. "And what business are you in?"

"Guitars," she answered.

"Is there anything I can do to help?"

"Only if you can tell us how to get to Liverpool…"

Just then Ben approached.

His conversation with Pittsburgh Guitars had gone well. Sam put him on the phone with the store's owner, John, who had performed in Liverpool a few years ago with his Beatles tribute band. John explained that the fastest way to England from France was the Chunnel. "But don't call it that, you'll sound like a tourist," he said. "The train that runs under the English Channel is the Eurostar." John told him that the Eurostar runs almost every hour and goes from the Gare du Nord train station in Paris to the St. Pancras station in London. And three blocks from the St. Pancras station in London is the Euston station, with trains to Liverpool.

Ben thanked John, and then googled Eurostar and booked two seats on the 7:55 am train. "Angie's not the only one who can make reservations on the fly," he said to himself.

Back at the table, Henri saw Ben heading toward them. He stood up and moved aside.

Not immediately aware of Henri's presence, Ben, proud of his booking accomplishment, said aloud to Angie, "We're on the 7:55 train!"

Looking up at Ben, and then Henri, Angie said, "Ben, this is Henri."

Henri nodded to Ben and said, *"Bonjour."* He then turned to Angie, reached out to shake her hand and said, "It was nice meeting you. I hope you find your guitar." And he was quickly gone among the crowd.

Sitting down next to Angie, Ben said, "What was that all about?"

"I'm not sure," she replied. "But in my sleepless state, I may have given away too much information."

"What do you mean?"

With a concerned look on her face she said, "I never told him we were looking for a guitar…"

Taking a moment to access the situation, Ben said, "Someone may be on to us. But there is nothing we can do until morning."

He smiled at her and said, "Don't worry about it. Let's have that drink."

An hour later they were both in their rooms at the hotel, and sound asleep.

***

Ben slept for ten hours. But the time difference had severely skewed their schedule. He was up, dressed and ready to go before 4 am. To pass the time he wandered down to the lobby of the hotel. Next to the registration desk was a small glassed-in room with a computer. The door read, *"Centre d'Affaires* – Business Center."

Time to learn about the mystery guitar they were tracking. He logged on and read everything he could about Gibson's 1958 "Modern Series" guitars. There were numerous pictures of original 1958 Flying Vs and Explorers, but no photos of the third model, now known as the Moderne. He found the patent drawing, though. And hundreds of pictures of various "reissues." At least now he'd recognize the shape of the guitar. And he noted that, just as Angie had explained, there were no controls or pickguard on the 1958 patent drawing. So the position of those items on the reissues were just conjecture. It would be interesting to see how the reissues compared to the original. Provided, of course, that they could find it.

During his internet searches Ben was particularly amused when he found a photo of Dave Davies in The Kinks playing a `58 Flying V. Unlike the many other photos of musicians holding that model, Dave played with his arm through the V-part of the guitar. This required him to hold the guitar higher, and position his right arm in a straight horizontal position. Uncomfortable, but very distinctive.

Ben was a Kinks fan in the mid-1970s when his band covered several of their songs. He loved the way Dave Davies played with unbridled passion and spirit. Now, sitting in a Business Center in a hotel in Paris almost forty-five years later, he read article after article about the group. He was surprised to read that the band's original bass player, Pete Quaife, passed away in 2010. Then he stumbled across a post written by Dave Davies, after Pete's death.

It read: "I am overwhelmed with emotion... Pete was right there at the very beginning... we might never have done any of this without him... A true artist and an immensely gifted man, who was never really given the credit he deserved for his contributions and involvement... I knew he was ill, but in my naivety I kind of thought we would work again together."

Ben was particularly struck by the last sentence. He knew that no one lives forever. But he realized that he, too, was naïve when it came to seeing his family and friends again. He presumed that when he needed them, they'd be there.

If this long-distance guitar quest ever ended he was going to tell everyone that he loved them. Maybe he'd even arrange a get-together with his old band mates...

Then his phone buzzed.

It was a text from Angie. She was awake and she would be ready to go in fifteen minutes.

As he stared down at the text, he smiled. He wasn't sure if he wanted this quest to end.

Chapter Thirty

The departure from Paris had been smooth. The Eurostar had airport-style security checkpoints, but the operation was quick and friendly. Ben and Angie easily made it to their assigned seats in Car #7. The high-speed Eurostar train would have them in London in a little over two hours.

After nearly an hour of French farmland speeding by their window, Angie volunteered to find breakfast, and she made her way to the food car, two train cars away. A quarter of the car was taken up by an enclosed cooking area where a very friendly Eurostar employee served Panini sandwiches and wine, coffee or soft drinks. The rest of the car had no seats, only high-top tables. Dozens of travelers stood around the car, chatting and eating.

As Angie juggled two sandwiches and two drinks, she turned to make her way back to Car #7. Then, across the crowd, she saw a familiar face. Entering the car from the opposite door was Henri, the man who had approached her the night before. Back in Paris he appeared to be just an innocent flirt making casual conversation. But what are the odds he would be on the same train to London early the next morning?

She ducked through the crowd before he saw her, and she hurried back to Ben.

"Remember the French Casanova?" she said, as she dropped into the seat next to Ben.

"The guy from yesterday?" said Ben.

"Yeah. He's here." She continued, "I knew there was something fishy about him."

"Is this guitar such a big deal that someone would follow us from Paris?" Ben asked, although he already knew the answer.

"We need a plan," said Angie.

Just then Ben's phone buzzed with a text from John at Pittsburgh Guitars.

"How is the trip going?" it said.

Ben replied, "On the Eurostar. Heading to London and then Liverpool."

He quickly calculated that it was 3 am back in Pittsburgh. He figured that John was just coming home from a gig with his band.

"Any further advice?" Ben texted.

"Take the Euston station train to Liverpool," John replied, "When you get to Liverpool, I recommend the Adelphi Hotel. It's only a block from the Lime Street train station. And it's famous. Or, if you want to be touristy, go to the Hard Day's Night Hotel on Matthew Street near The Cavern."

Ben was vaguely familiar with The Cavern, the basement club where the Beatles got their start.

"Thanks!" he wrote back. "We'll be in touch!"

He turned to Angie and continued their conversation. "I was pretty groggy last night, but if I remember, you told Henri where we were going, right? And then I told him we were taking this train?"

Embarrassed, Angie said, "Yes. But in our defense, we were exhausted…"

Shaking his head and glancing down at his phone, Ben said, "It's not our fault. We're not used to being international jet-setting guitar hunters. Now we just need to lose him. But, he knows we're going to Liverpool, so we won't be able to ditch him until we get there."

As they chatted Ben barely noticed that the sunlight outside their windows had vanished. By the time he realized that they must be in a tunnel, it was light again. Presuming they were still in France, he glanced out the window and noticed that the street signage was now in English. "Was *that* the English Channel?" he thought to himself. He had wondered if he'd be nervous as the train went under the water. But that part of the trip was so fast that he missed it.

Less than a half hour later the train arrived at the St. Pancras Station in London, and in a few minutes they were off the train and on the street.

A street vendor directed them to head west, and a quick three-block walk brought them to the London Euston train station, which was huge. As a hub, there were trains leaving for destinations all around England. It was also a main subway stop. Surrounding the two-story lobby were shops and restaurants.

Ben said, "I'll get the tickets." He pointed to a pub on the second floor with a balcony view of the entire lobby. "I'll meet you up there. Keep an eye out for our mystery man."

By the time Ben returned with the tickets Angie was already nursing a beer. Moments later she pointed down to the lobby.

There he was.

As they watched, Henri looked up at the giant electronic train schedule board and checked his watch. Ben said to Angie, "I think we can rule out coincidence. He must be working for the *Guitare Occasion* shop in Paris. And he's going to try to get to the guitar before we do."

"Well, at least he doesn't know that we know he's here," said Angie.

"Right," said Ben. "And let's keep it that way."

More than a dozen tracks lead from the Euston Station. Shortly before boarding time, the electronic board indicated that the Liverpool train would be leaving from Track 14. Ben and Angie made their way down to the train platform and as they were walking, Ben turned to Angie.

"I have an idea," he said. "Let Henri see us but pretend you don't see him. We'll get him to follow us."

177

They positioned themselves ten or twenty people in front of Henri, and they all boarded the train.

Once aboard, Ben and Angie settled into their seats for a trip that would actually take longer than the trip from Paris, albeit at a slower speed.

As Ben intently pulled up different web sites on his cell phone, Angie said, "Are you going to lead him astray?"

"That's my plan," said Ben. "And after this search is over I'm going to work on you."

She laughed and said, "Well, *that* will be an interesting trip."

Ben was busy on the internet for much of the train ride to Liverpool. Angie could see his mind racing, so she didn't interrupt. When they arrived at the Lime Street Station in Liverpool, Ben said, "We're going to get a cab. Make sure that he's still following us."

Next to the Lime Street Station was a line of traditional British black taxi cabs. They walked slowly toward the cabs, giving Henri time to seemingly secretly trail them.

Entering the cab, Ben said, "The Hard Day's Night Hotel, please."

Angie looked at him. "So, we're taking the tourist route?"

"So it would seem," Ben said, intently.

Ten minutes later they were entering the newly designed Hard Day's Night Hotel.

The hotel lobby featured floor to ceiling pictures of The Beatles as well as a juke box constantly playing their songs. Off to the right was the check-in desk, and to the left, the hotel bar. Ben handed their bags to Angie and said, "You wait in the bar and keep an eye out. I'm going to look at the juke box until Henri shows up. Text me when you see him."

Angie positioned herself in the bar so that she could see the front of the hotel. Moments later a taxi arrived with Henri. As Ben felt the vibration of Angie's text in his pocket, he walked to the check-in desk and requested a room.

Angie could see him not only signing for the room, but also discussing something else with the desk clerk. She saw the clerk reach for a nearby newspaper and flip through its pages. Ben then made another request and Angie saw the desk clerk make some notes.

Wrapping up the interaction, Ben took the room keys, turned and walked straight to the bar to join Angie. "Let's order a drink," he said.

"I couldn't help myself," she smiled, "Two martinis are already on the way." They sipped their drinks and tried to act nonchalant, all the while keeping an eye on the Frenchman wandering around the lobby.

Eventually Henri made his way to the check-in desk. He, too, had a long-winded conversation with the desk clerk.

A few minutes later they saw Henri take the elevator up to his room. Pushing the half-finished drinks away, Ben grabbed their bags. "Let's go," he said, motioning to the bar's side door, leading to the street. Angie nodded, with a fake serious look on her face. Inside she was enjoying the subterfuge.

In moments they were back out on Matthew Street. Ben held up his arm to flag down a cab and Angie followed silently. Climbing into the back of the large black taxi, Ben said, "The Adlephi Hotel, please."

Once they were safely in the back of the car, Angie laughed and said, "Pretty smooth. I feel like a secret agent. What exactly happened?"

"Well," Ben explained, "Philippe at Oldies Guitars told us that the guitar ended up with Conor Kelly in the band The Stormers. But the guys across the street at *Guitar Occasion* only knew the purchaser, Mrs. Beauchamp, and, thanks to us, the fact that it's in Liverpool. So, to Henri the guitar could be with any band in this town. He'd have to follow us to find it.

"On the train I searched the internet for 1960's bands that were still actively performing. Then I checked all of their schedules to see if any of them were out of town tonight. And I found one. The Merseybeats. They're playing in Manchester this evening. That's an hour-and-a-half away, northeast from here.

"When I checked into the hotel I told the clerk behind the counter that we came to town just to see The Merseybeats, and could he tell me where they were performing. He looked them up in a local music magazine and told me that they'd be in Manchester tonight. I then told him that it was *very* important that we see them, and I asked him to book train tickets for us to Manchester.

"My guess was that Henri would think of some way to figure out where we were going. Maybe he would say he was a friend of ours, or something. If he was able to track us down in Paris, he'd be able to track our next steps here, as well. And as we watched from the bar, I could tell that the clerk made train reservations for him, too.

"If all goes according to plan, in an hour he'll be on a train to Manchester. It will take him most of the afternoon to ride to Manchester, track down the band, realize that they don't have the guitar, and then take the train back. Hopefully that will buy us enough time to find Conor Kelly.

"And I'm moving us to The Adelphi to say out of Henri's way."

"I'm impressed!" said Angie.

"Hey, I've learned a few things in the cut-throat insurance biz," he said smiling. "Well, from that and all of the spy movies I've watched!"

"Ah… I see…" she laughed. "Well done, 007."

A few minutes later their taxi was pulling up in front of the Adelphi Hotel.

"Time to get to work," Ben said, as he helped Angie out of the taxi and carried their bags to reception.

Chapter Thirty-One

"The Stormers? Let me check the paper."

"I appreciate that," Ben said to the Adelphi Hotel receptionist, "But they don't have a gig until next weekend. I was just wondering if you knew anyone from the band..."

"Sorry, I don't. A bit too young, I'm afraid," she replied. "But I know who would. Millie, the hotel manager. I'll ring her."

"That would be great," said Ben.

Looking over his shoulder he saw Angie climbing the eight steps that led from the hotel foyer to the massive Grand Ballroom.

Turning back to the receptionist, he said, "We'll be up there."

A moment later he was standing next to Angie, staring up at the huge ceiling with decorative glass panels and oversize chandeliers. Around the hall, large marble columns were built into the walls. It was the most elaborate room Ben had ever seen.

"Imagine the parties and events that have been held here," she said.

"A hundred years ago the hotel was a major departure point for wealthy folks heading to America," said a soft English voice from behind them. "At one time the world's biggest ocean liners left from Liverpool, and they held bon voyage parties here. Hi, I'm Millie, the hotel manager," she said.

Millie was a petite, gray haired lady with a kind, warm smile.

"It's so nice to meet you," said Angie, shaking her hand. "I'm Angie and this is Ben. And I'm sure it's obvious from our accents that we're from America. My father passed through Liverpool on his way home from World War II. I wonder if he ever made it into the hotel."

181

"Ah," Millie laughed. "I was just a small child, but I remember there were soldiers *everywhere* after the War. And now, it's so many years later. My, how the time goes on…"

"At least *we're* still here," Angie said smiling.

"Well, the building is looking good," said Millie, gesturing around the room. "I'm not so sure about myself," she said with a smile.

"Ha! You look fabulous," said Angie.

"That's so kind of you. Now, I understand you're looking for The Stormers?"

"Actually, only one of them. Conor Kelly. Do you know him?"

Millie smiled again. "I've known him my entire life," she said. "The Stormers were *very* popular in the early `60s. They'd often play the afternoon session at The Cavern and I would run down there on my lunch break from work. They're still a great band."

"Would there be any chance of you arranging a meeting with us?" Angie asked.

"Let me call Conor on my mobile," Millie replied.

As Millie stepped away from them to make the call, Angie turned to Ben and said, "Everyone in this town is so friendly."

"Maybe it's the music," said Ben.

***

"You're in luck. Conor is visiting a friend in the city. He'll meet you at The Cavern at half past seven. I told him to look for the attractive girl and a reasonable-looking man with the white tennis shoes. Conor said he'd be the one holding a pint of Guinness," she laughed.

"You are wonderful," said Angie. "I hope we meet again!"

"Take care," said Millie. "And watch out for *this* guy," she said pointing toward Ben.

As Mille walked off, Ben said to Angie, "Yep, that's what it is. There is so much music in this city that everyone has an air of happiness around them."

Looking at the time on his cell phone, he said, "We have a couple of hours to kill. Let's check into our rooms and then get some dinner. And we have to keep an eye out for Henri, so let's stick close to the hotel."

***

Thirty minutes later they were standing in front of the hotel. Looking to the right, they noticed an Irish pub next door.

"Fish and chips?" he asked.

"And a pint?" Angie replied.

They found a table in the back of the pub, where they could watch the door. The Manchester train reservations that Ben made at The Hard Day's Night Hotel were for the 6 pm departure. Hopefully, Henri would be on that train, beginning his wild-goose chase. Until then, they would be cautious.

***

Ben knew that 'fish and chips' were fried fish with french fries, but he was surprised to see that the meal came with a side of mushy peas. Referring back to the menu, he saw that they were actually called 'mushy peas.' "Well, the menu warned me," he thought to himself, smiling.

Sliding the peas aside, he looked over at Angie and said, "We're really wrapped up in history on this trip. We're staying at a hundred-year-old hotel, trying to track down a mythical guitar, which is currently in the hands of a musician who was famous fifty years ago."

"History is what we're trying to make on this trip," she replied. "This guitar will change the history of electric guitars."

"Will we be famous?" he asked waving a french fry.

183

"I doubt it. But Red Brown might be."

"But he's not around to enjoy it…" said Ben.

"Well, people will remember his name. And isn't that all any of us can hope for? That people will remember us when we're gone?" She suddenly seemed a bit melancholy.

In an effort to change the topic, Ben said, "Hey, how many guitars did you own at your peak?"

"Oh, I don't know… a couple of hundred, maybe," she answered.

"And how many do you have now?" he asked.

"Seven… no, six. I sold that Martin to Dusty."

"Don't you miss them?"

"Remember the dealers we met at the Philly guitar show?" she said. "Those guys fell in love with the electric guitar as teenagers in the 1960s. They're in the business for the love of the instrument. And it's worked out well for them. I honestly think a lot of them would do it for nothing, just to be around guitars…"

She glanced off. "They're good guys. I love 'em." Then laughing, she added, "Well, *most* of them!"

Getting back to her story, she said, "But the truth is that I'm not like them. I didn't see The Beatles on Ed Sullivan. I didn't buy a cheap guitar, take lessons and immediately form a garage band. And I didn't spend my teens wishing I could afford a real Strat. I *do* know a lot about guitars. And I've made a *lot* of money with guitars. But eventually it was time to clean house."

"Well, I could never part with Aunt Maggie's Strat," he replied. "And I'd never sell Bob Stewart's bass. They mean too much to me."

"And that's *exactly* when you should keep a guitar," she said. "When it's worth more to you than the money."

"Hey," she added, checking her phone, "It's time to get going.

Chapter Thirty-Two

They grabbed a taxi and headed down to the famous Cavern Club. Since Mathew Street, where The Cavern is located, is a pedestrian-only road, the taxi dropped them off at the end of the block, right back in front of the Hard Day's Night Hotel.

Looking around for any sign of Henri, Ben said, "This could have been awkward!"

Also looking around, Angie said, "I think your diversion plan worked." Just the same, they hurried down Mathew Street.

A circular staircase with black walls led them down into the club. Directly beyond the entrance was a bar and off to their left, across the room was a small stage. Looking toward the stage they could see that the ceiling was three arched sections, with the wider section in the center. The arched ceiling and the pillars supporting it, as well as the walls, were made of faded red brick. The narrower arched sections on either side had tables and chairs, while center was open, for either a standing or dancing crowd. On stage a band was setting up their equipment. Early-1960s rock and roll was blasting from the sound system.

Twenty or thirty people were in the club, but Angie quickly made eye contact with a 75-year-old gentleman at the bar. True to his word, he was holding a pint of Guinness.

"Welcome to Liverpool," he said, "I'm Conor Kelly."

Leaning in close so that he could hear her over the music, Angie introduced herself. Conor nodded, and said, "Come this way."

Parallel to the bar was a hallway that led to a larger, much quieter back room. This room had a stage that was easily three times as large as the other. There were rows of tables, and a much larger bar. A few customers wandered about.

"Out front is the classic room," he said. "It's not the original, but very close. They use this back room for bigger shows."

As the three of them sat down he motioned to the bartender to bring two more beers.

"So, I can't imagine that you two are Stormers fans from the States. But Millie liked you, and that's good enough for me. What can I do for you?"

For the next five minutes Ben laid out the story, from Aunt Maggie, to the shady dealer visiting Ruth Brown right after her husband's funeral, convincing her that he would get the guitar appraised, to Ben and Angie's international quest to find the guitar.

"You've come a long way," said Conor. "This guitar must be important."

"It's important on many levels," said Angie.

"Well, it *was* a gift from Natalie. But she's just trying to buy my affection, if you know what I mean," he said, laughing. "To be honest, I don't really care for the guitar. The arm is too fat."

Ben wondered what he meant, but then as Conor lifted his left hand in a playing position Ben realized that he was referring to the guitar's neck. Ben nodded.

Conor continued, "I told Natalie Beauchamp that I wanted an Explorer, so she bought me this. It was the closest we could find. And the cost meant nothing to her. Meanwhile, this week, Curly's got in a new Explorer. I was planning to go there tomorrow to trade it in."

"Curly's?" asked Ben.

"Curly Music, up on Ranelagh Street. Near the Adelphi," he replied. "But now that I know that the guitar is of questionable origin, it should probably go back to its true owner…"

"How about this plan?" said Angie. "First thing tomorrow we will buy the Explorer at Curly's and trade it to you for the old guitar."

"Hmmm," said Conor, as he considered the deal, "I think that would work for me."

"I can't thank you enough for this," said Ben. "Is there *anything* we can do to repay you?"

"Ha!" said Conor. "Nothing that's possible. I've been around for a lot of years, and I've had some wonderful times. I wouldn't change any of it except for one thing. A guitar I gave away in 1965. I had it when we first formed the band and I loved it. All of my early musical memories are attached to that guitar. But it's long gone."

"What guitar was it?" asked Angie.

"It was a Les Paul. It's probably in the States now. But so are a million other Les Pauls."

"What happened to it?" asked Ben.

"When The Beatles made it in America, many of the rest of us thought we could, too. But without the right management and a big record label behind you, that's a hard thing to do. After a month of bad gigs in the States we ran out of money. We all came home except our other guitar player, Legs Jones. I left the guitar with him."

"Legs?" said Angie, smiling.

Conor laughed out loud. "Yeah. He got more girls than anyone else in the band, but he spent most of his time running away from their boyfriends!"

He continued, "I didn't see him again for three years. By that time he had sold the guitar."

"Was it gold?" ask Angie, wondering if it was a mid-1950's Les Paul goldtop.

"Yeah," said Conor. "With two black pickups."

187

That combination puzzled Angie, but rather than question further she asked, "Do you have a picture?"

Much to her surprise, he said "I think there's one here."

He yelled over to the bar, "Frankie, do you have that *History of The Cavern* book?"

"Sure," said Frankie, "I'll bring one over. Do you want another pint?"

"The book and the drink, please," said Conor.

Frankie delivered a Guinness and the book. Conor opened it and paged halfway through. There, at the top of page 20, was a black and white photo of the Stormers on the Cavern stage in 1963. They were dressed in grey suits with skinny black ties. The audience was wall-to-wall girls and they were screaming for the band. Based on the look of both the band and the audience, Angie guessed that it must have been 100 degrees in the club that night.

"Those were some fantastic times," said Conor, looking sentimentally at the photo. "I know you can't go back. But I've often thought that if I had that guitar, I'd have a memory that I could touch."

Angie tilted the book to get a little more light on the photo. Ten seconds later Ben and Conor saw her smile from ear to ear.

She looked at them both and excitedly said, "I know that guitar!"

"How is that possible?" said Ben in disbelief.

"That's no ordinary Les Paul," she said. "It has two P-90 pickups, with the black plastic covers. But if you look closely at the photo you can see that the pickup covers have little tabs on either side, attaching the pickups to the guitar."

"So?" asked Ben.

"So Gibson made two flat-body electric guitars like this in the 1950s, the Les Paul Special, with two P-90s and the Les Paul Junior with one P-90. But on the Special, the pickups were attached with two screws going down the center of the pickups. On the one-pickup Junior, the pickup cover attached with tabs on the sides. Like this. This guitar, Conor's guitar, was originally a Les Paul Junior and someone added a second pickup.

"Furthermore, the Junior only had two knobs, a volume and a tone. If you look at the photo you can see that someone added a toggle switch between those two knobs, as a pickup selector."

"I wondered why my guitar only had two controls, when Legs' two-pickup Gibson had four." said Conor.

"And on top of that," Angie added, "someone added a Bigsby vibrato.

"Oh, right," said Conor. "A friend helped me do that on the counter at Hessy's music store."

She stared at the picture again. "I know exactly where this guitar is."

Conor stared at her, almost in shock. He finally spoke, "I will pay whatever it takes to get that guitar back. I don't care if the guitar that Natalie bought for me, the one I'm giving back to you, is worth a million pounds, it can't buy the memories I have with my old Les Paul."

Pulling out her cell phone, Angie said, "Hold that thought."

Angie dialed a number. Ben and Conor could only hear her side of the conversation.

"Dusty! Do you still have that modified TV Junior? The one with the added pickup, added toggle, and Bigsby?"

They could see her smile.

"Yeah, yeah, I know...It's your favorite guitar..." she said sarcastically.

"How much do you want for it?...Yeah, I know it would be worth twice as much without the modifications...But how much do you *really* want for it?..."

She winked and held up a finger to Ben and Conor, as if to say, "This will only take a minute."

Angie continued, "Dusty, consider this a personal favor to me. What's the best you can do on it? Perfect. I'll take it. I'll text you a shipping address in a little while...By the way, it's going to England...Yes, I'll cover the shipping...Yes, I'm in England now...I'll explain when I get back...No, you're married now, remember?... Okay, Bye... Love you, too."

Conor looked at her, not knowing what to think. "I'm speechless," he said.

"Ben and I are going to cover this," she said. "No charge for the guitar or the memories."

She could see a tear in his eye.

"By returning Red Brown's guitar you are going to change someone's life. The least we can do is help you with *your* quest," said Angie. "Besides, some guitars, like some memories, are worth more than money."

As they stood up to leave, Conor said, "I'm *really* going to have to thank Millie for this meeting."

"You should ask her out," said Angie.

Conor smiled. "An old man like me?" he said.

"You still have some new memories to make," Angie replied.

"So," said Ben, "Can we meet in the lobby of The Adelphi tomorrow at 11 am? We'll have the Explorer."

"That *and* you're sending the Les Paul? I don't know what to say?" said Conor. "But I'll be there with the guitar."

"Great!" said Ben.

"By the way," Conor added, "The guitar only has a cheap gig bag. There's no real case."

"I know," said Angie. "That's not a problem."

Chapter Thirty-Three

11:15 am.

For the fourth time in ten minutes, Ben checked his phone.

He and Angie were sitting in the lobby of The Adelphi Hotel in Liverpool. An hour ago they walked a block-and-a-half down Ranelagh Street to Curly Music, where they purchased a two-year-old white Gibson Explorer. Ben was originally concerned that it wasn't the one Conor Kelly wanted, but the salesman at Curly's assured them that it was the only Explorer to pass through the shop in months.

Now Ben's concern was whether Conor would show up to make the trade. Last night it crossed his mind that they should go right to Conor's house to get the guitar. But at the time they didn't have the Explorer to trade, and as nice as Conor was, it seemed unlikely that he would just hand over the instrument that Natalie Beauchamp had purchased for him in Paris.

Ben got up and walked to the front door of the hotel. The Adelphi sat on one of the higher areas in Liverpool. From the hotel the rest of the town sloped down toward the Mersey River. He remembered the old song, "Ferry Cross The Mersey," by Gerry and The Pacemakers. He was now less than a mile from the ferry and the river, but like so many other locations here and in Paris, he and Angie had been too busy to take in the tourist sights. "Someday…" he thought. Meanwhile, where was Conor?

Just as Ben pulled out his phone to check the time again, Millie, the hotel manager, walked over to him. Sensing his concern, she said, "Don't worry about Conor. He's a musician. You can't expect him to be on time this early in the morning."

Ben laughed.

"I spoke with him last night," she continued. "He was quite in shock that you found his old Les Paul. He's been talking about that guitar for fifty years."

Turning back to face the door, Ben smiled. "It was all Angie's doing," he said.

For that matter, he thought, the entire trip was Angie's doing. Certainly Ben was anxious to help Red Brown's widow, but without Angie he'd still be sitting in her kitchen in Bethlehem, PA, wondering where to start. In fact, he probably wouldn't have even made it to Ruth Brown's house. He'd most likely still be at his desk in Pittsburgh.

For a brief moment he wondered if the guitar was worth the trouble and expense that they'd gone to. But he quickly realized that it *had* been worth it, even if just for the thrill of the search. He had been pushing himself to the limit physically and emotionally, but he loved every minute of it.

He was suddenly shaken out of his mental ramblings when he saw two men, one with a guitar gig bag slung over his shoulder, walking up Lime Street toward the hotel.

Pushing open the hotel door to get a better look, he was shocked to see Conor with Henri, the man who had followed them from Paris. As they walked, Henri was speaking emphatically, with numerous arm gestures. Conor calmly walked beside him, smiling. Ben was tempted to run down the steps of the hotel to interrupt the conversation, when he saw them come to a stop. Conor held out his hand to shake Henri's, he nodded, and then turned toward the hotel. Henri was still speaking as Conor walked away. Although Ben could not hear what was being said, Henri's words turned into shouting. Without turning back, Conor held up his hand as if to wave goodbye.

A few moments later, Conor was at the door. Ben held it for him as he entered.

"Good morning ladies," he said as he saw Millie and Angie in the lobby.

Turning to Ben, he pointed with his thumb out to the street and said, "Quite an insistent gentleman."

Ben was speechless.

Conor continued, "He didn't want to give me any information about the guitar. Only that he would pay anything to get it. *Anything.*"

He reached out to pat Ben on the shoulder. "What he didn't understand is that money is not the most important thing in the world."

Angie opened the hard-shell rectangular case of the Explorer and handed the guitar to Conor. He sat down in the chair next to her and played the intro to "Johnny B. Goode." She was surprised at the speed of his aging fingers.

"Oh, this will be a fun guitar," he said, looking up at Millie, who was standing there, smiling at him.

Angie then held up her phone to display a photo. Conor turned toward her and stared at the screen intently.

"Dusty sent me a photo of the Les Paul," she said. "That's the one, right?"

Conor looked at the photo with a tear in his eye.

"Yes. Yes, that's it. I can't believe it."

"Great," she said, "Give me your address and it will be here in three days."

"I can't thank you enough," said Conor, handing her the gig bag to complete the exchange. "I hope you make a lot of money with this."

"It's not for Ben and me," she said. "But as I mentioned last night, it's going to change the life of its real owner."

From a few feet away Ben watched her gingerly accept the gig bag from Conor. Angie had spent thousands of dollars on plane tickets, $500 on a Hofner Bass kit that was being shipped to a friendly guitar store in Paris, over a thousand dollars on the Explorer at Curly's, and who knows how much buying the Les Paul from Dusty, all to help Red Brown's family...and along the way, see and touch this famous, yet unknown guitar. She was truly an unusual person.

Angie unzipped the gig bag carefully. He could see a large, oddly shaped headstock as she removed the guitar from the case. She let the case fall to the floor and laid the guitar in her lap. Shaking her head, she stared at it. To no one in particular she said, "Wow."

The guitar was a light colored Korina wood, just like the photos of the 1958 Flying Vs and Explorers Ben had seen on the internet in Paris. The gold on the hardware had slightly faded but was still intact. Ben remembered that Red didn't receive the guitar until the early 1960s, so it had been handled at the Gibson factory for several years. That accounted for several nicks and scratches. The entire guitar had the odd look of something that was over 60 years old, yet still in excellent condition.

Angie looked up at him and said, "Look. No one guessed right on the pickguard."

Ben smiled at her with an amused look on his face.

"The patent drawings didn't show the pickguard," she said. "Ibanez was the first company make a reissue of this, in 1975, and they guessed that the pickguard had a big sloping curve and covered most of the body. When Gibson finally did their official reissue in 1982, *they* guessed that the pickguard was very small. But, look! They were both wrong," she said holding up the guitar.

The white pickguard was shaped like a wide, fat, upside-down V. The shorter front leg ended at the lower cutaway. The pickguard then angled up between the pickups, peaked above and halfway between the

194

bridge and the tailpiece, and then angled down toward the bottom left part of the guitar.

"It's much more space-age looking than anyone imagined," she said. "And, of course, that *was* the point of the three Modern models…to be new, innovative, 1958-era-space-age instruments. Red Brown did a good job."

Although Ben, Conor and Millie were all looking at her, no one really understood what she meant. At least not on Angie's level. But she was clearly very excited and emotional about the guitar.

"I'm glad you're happy," said Conor.

"Oh, I am!" said Angie, cradling the guitar to her chest.

Reaching out to shake Millie's and then Conor's hand, Ben said, "It was very nice to meet you both. Thank you so much. I'm sorry we can't stay."

"Be sure to come back and visit," said Conor.

"Yes, and you have to see Conor's band. They're wonderful!" said Millie.

Conor put his arm around her, and said to Ben, "She still sees me as a twenty-year-old."

Angie quickly re-packed the old guitar in its gig bag. She threw it over her shoulder and grabbed the suitcase sitting on the floor next to her.

Looking at her phone, she said, "Ben and I have to run. If we hurry we can make the next train."

She nodded to Ben to grab his suitcase, and then hugged Millie and Conor, saying, "It was lovely meeting you."

The Lime Street Station was only a long block-and-a-half away, but they took one of the taxis in front of the hotel anyway, both for speed and to avoid any potential meeting with Henri. They had only arrived from London yesterday. Now, instead of heading back to London, they were

195

taking a train to Manchester, the nearest city with an international flight back to America.

Once inside the station Ben looked up at the multiple train schedule boards. He saw that earlier that morning there had been a 9:04 train to London. He was suddenly overcome with sentimental memories of his band from four decades earlier. They used to play the Beatles song, "One After 909." Although he sang the lead, he had never paid much attention to the lyrics. But now, there on the board he saw the 9:04. Back in The Beatles' day it was probably the 9:09. And today, below the 9:04 listing was the 9:47 train... The "one after 9:04."

It was a seemingly inconsequential thought. But the magic of it all washed over him. That many years ago The Beatles had written a song about a train leaving from this very station, the next train after the 9:09 train... the one after 9:09... And *then*, ten years later Ben sang the song with his band in Pittsburgh... And *now*, he was standing there.

An assortment of feelings collided in his head. He missed his band. He missed hurrying to the record store to buy a new album. He missed playing the songs over and over to work out the guitar parts. He missed the innocence of the times. The innocence of his youth. As he stood there in the middle of a train station, he completely understood everything Conor Kelly had said to them.

Moments later he felt Angie tugging at his arm. "Come on, we're on Track 4."

***

They didn't say much to each other on the hour-and-twenty-minute ride to the Manchester International Airport. Angie still couldn't believe that the Modern 3, formerly known as the Moderne, actually existed. And that it was currently in her arms. Ben couldn't take his eyes off of her. She was so happy. And being near her, so was he.

***

The airport was hectic, but Angie made her way to the ticket counter. Twenty minutes later she returned.

"Well, that wasn't easy... There was a lot of explaining to do, buying three one-way tickets, at the last minute, and one of the tickets is for an inanimate object."

She held up the tickets. "So, be prepared to be stared at. But we're on our way, and the Modern 3 has its own seat. After all we've been through, it's not going to leave our sight."

The flight home was long, but they had plenty of time to re-live every detail of their 67-hour trip overseas. They laughed about all of the classic sights they had missed. They laughed that they still had tickets home from Paris on a different airline. They laughed at what little sleep they had. And they laughed as they tried to explain to the flight attendants why there was a guitar seat-belted into the seat beside them. "On a flight this long I hope he doesn't get a stiff neck," Ben said, pointing at the guitar. It seemed funny at the time.

***

As the flight finally approached Pittsburgh, Angie said, "When we get home, you take the guitar. You have the case anyway. Call Ruth to see what she'd like to do. We can drive it back to her, or if she wants to sell it, I know some trustworthy people who can handle that for her."

An hour later they were back at their respective homes. Later that night he picked up the old photo that his dad had given him, the promo picture of Aunt Maggie's band. He looked at the young, enthusiastic faces of his aunt and her three band mates. The picture had faded, but the smiles were still there.

"Well, Maggie," he said, "You asked me to help Red with his guitar. I was a little late for Red. But I think I'll be able to help his family. And your daughter."

He smiled and put the photo down.

Then he added, "And you'll be happy to know that you've helped me, too."

He looked at the guitar cases leaning in the corner of his living room. Maggie's Stratocaster. Bob Stewart's Gibson bass. Red Brown's Modern 3, now safely stored in its original case.

And at the front of the row, his old Melody Maker. The least valuable of the group, by a long shot. Just the same, he opened the case and took the guitar out. And played "One After 909."

Chapter Thirty-Four

Ruth Brown was thrilled to hear that Ben and Angie found Red's old guitar.

She wanted all of the details of their adventure, often interrupting with an "Oh, my!" She told Ben that Red never played the guitar, and she felt no emotional attachment to it. She asked if Ben could sell it for her. And she wanted to make sure that he and Angie were compensated for all their expenses. "Hopefully there will be some money left over for Elizabeth," she said, referring to her adopted daughter, Ben's cousin. "I have a feeling you'll be pleasantly surprised," said Ben.

He called Angie and told her the guitar was on the market.

As word spread through the vintage guitar community, the initial reaction was one of skepticism. But once it was clear that Ben and Angie not only had the guitar with its original case, but also the long-lost Gibson log book which itemized all of the "Modern Series" guitars made in 1958, along with their respective serial numbers, the doubt turned to excitement.

After the whirlwind weekend in Paris and Liverpool tracking down the guitar, Ben and Angie were now faced with a whirlwind of offers. Ben took more time off from his job, as he and Angie plotted the best move for Red Brown's family. Angie knew from personal experience that there are collectors who will pay shocking amounts of money for rare vintage guitars. And there was no rarer guitar than the instrument now known as the *Modern 3*. After four days of fielding phone calls and emails from all over the world, they decided that placing it up for auction was the wisest move.

Out of fear that the guitar might disappear forever after the auction, Angie arranged to have every inch of it photographed and documented. And every page of the Log Book was copied.

"Some wealthy person is going to keep this guitar in their collection, which is fine," she said. "But I want the true information about it to be out there, available to everyone."

Arrangements were made with a major auction house in Manhattan. A date was set and Ben safely delivered the guitar to New York, once again buying a separate seat for it on the flight from Pittsburgh. He then returned to Pittsburgh and his job where he faced a pile of unfinished documents stacked on his desk.

With a week to wait, Angie flew to Nashville to thank Dusty for his help and pay for the Les Paul he sent to Conor in Liverpool.

When the auction date arrived, Ben flew to New York from Pittsburgh. Ruth was not feeling well enough to make the trip, but Elizabeth and her son Steve, the boy who answered the door when Ben and Angie finally found Red Brown's house, drove in from Bethlehem. Angie flew up from Nashville.

Just as Angie predicted, the guitar created a major stir in the vintage instrument market. Buyers phoned in bids from around the globe. As Angie, Ben, Elizabeth and Steve sat there in awe the bids climbed and climbed, finally settling at $5.6 million. The highest price ever paid for an electric guitar.

Elizabeth cried as she hugged Angie and Ben. "How can I ever thank you? You've changed our lives forever."

"It was your mother's note that got everything started," Ben replied, with a slight tear in his eye as well.

"Thank you, thank you, thank you," said Elizabeth as she and Steve headed to their car.

Turning to Angie, Ben said, "Well, what now?"

"I'll meet you back in Pittsburgh in a couple of days," she said. "I have to go to Harrisburg to thank an old friend."

Ben remembered. Angie's friend Jeffery owned a pawn shop there, and she had called him from Paris asking him to ship a Hofner Bass kit.

Seeing the disappointed look in his eye, Angie smiled, reached out and touched his arm, and said, "Hey, when I get back to town, let's go out on a real date."

Ben smiled back at her. He would enjoy that.

Chapter Thirty-Five

Back in Pittsburgh, Ben put in his two weeks notice at work. He didn't have a plan for the future, but after everything he had experienced these last few weeks, he knew he didn't want to spend any more of his life behind that desk.

Two days later Angie called. "I'm back. How about tonight? For our date."

"Wear something nice," he said. "I'll pick you up at 6."

As Ben was walking out his door at 5:30, he ran into a FedEx delivery man coming up his sidewalk. The delivery man carried two registered envelopes addressed to Ben. He signed for them and hurriedly put them in his pocket. Remembering Angie's philosophy "If you're not five minutes early, you're late," he decided to get to Angie's house first, and then worry about the envelopes.

She met him at the door wearing a red dress, and for the first time since he met her, some jewelry. "You look wonderful!" he blurted out, surprising even himself.

"Come on in for a minute," she said.

"I've got nothing but time," he said. "I quit my job this week."

He could tell she was a little surprised, but she obviously approved. "Well, you didn't like it there anyway, right? Don't worry, I'll pay for dinner."

Noticing the two envelopes sticking out of his coat pocket, she asked, "What are those?"

In his rush to meet Angie, he had forgotten about them. He opened the first one.

The letter inside said: "I hope this covers your expenses. Love, Ruth."

Attached to the back of the letter was a check made out to 'Benjamin Cooper & Angie Addams.'

Ben looked at the check and laughed. "I guess we can *both* pay for dinner," he said handing her the check. The amount on the check was $10,000.

She looked at the check and smiled.

"It looks like we'll have to open a joint bank account," she said, grinning.

"And I thought we were just going out for dinner…" he said, smiling back at her.

Reaching for the second envelope, he said, "It will be hard to top that one."

This envelope also contained a letter. It read: "Ben and Angie, I can't thank you enough for what you have done for Red and me, and Elizabeth and Steve. Maggie would be so proud of you. Love, Ruth."

Attached to this letter was another check. But when he saw this one, Ben's face turned serious. He silently handed it to Angie. Once again it was made out to 'Benjamin Cooper & Angie Addams,' but the number featured many more zeros. The amount was $560,000.

As Ben stood there in shock, Angie put the check down, and put on her coat. Casually she said, "Relax, we'll put it in our new account."

Sliding her arm through his, she pointed them toward the door.

"What does this all mean?" he asked, still not believing the turn his life had taken since Aunt Maggie's Stratocaster arrived.

"It means we'll have some cash for our *next* adventure," Angie replied. "Now, how about that date?"

• • •

Made in the USA
Middletown, DE
01 December 2019

79801969R00117